I0733709

Caleb

His Defenders

Book 3

By

Ronna M. Bacon

Copyright © 2023 Ronna M. Bacon
ISBN 978-1-998821-17-4

Exodus 14:14. The Lord will fight for you, and you have only to be silent.

NKJV

Table of Contents

Tugging the ball cap further down over his dark brown curls, Caleb Campion stared around the parking lot that he had stopped in. Locking his truck door, he walked away, shifting the back pack to a more comfortable position on his shoulder. He had taken off that Saturday, just to hike some of the Niagara Peninsula, something that he liked to do when he needed to destress. That was something he really needed that weekend.

His dark brown eyes searched the area around him. He was uncomfortable as he strode forward, the sun just rising over the horizon. Early morning hikes suited him just fine. Today, though, he could feel someone watching him and he didn't like that. Not one bit.

Heading away from the parking lot, Caleb listened to the sounds of nature as the daytime critters and birds awoke and started with their songs and chirps. He drew in a deep breath. He had a feeling that something bad was about to happen to him. And that troubled him. He certainly did not want to face the danger that two of the men on their security team had faced.

Caleb paused for a moment, a hand held to an ear. He was hearing things, he decided. He was not hearing a lady's voice muttering away and off to the side of the trail. Shaking his head, Caleb moved forward, coming to a stop once more as the voice became somewhat louder.

Who is this, Lord? And why me? Did I really hear a lady's voice? And if I did, I just can't walk away from her. Yet, I don't know exactly where she is.

Taking a step forward, Caleb's head twisted as he sought to find the direction of the voice. He nodded before he walked to his left, finding a small pathway that he had not noticed before. The voice became louder. As it did, he frowned. Caleb could hear the pain in it and also a trace of tears. He paused as he came to a small clearing, not really that big, and searched it. His eyes landed on a lady who was seated on a log, one of her legs straight out in front of her.

Praying for her without knowing her or what she was going through, Caleb stepped forward. A small sound alerted the lady that she was not alone and she gave a small scream, her deep green eyes huge in her fear.

"Who are you? And where did you come from?" Her voice shook with her fear even as she tried to control it.

"I'm sorry. I didn't mean to startle you. I heard you and thought maybe you could use some help. If you don't, that's okay. I can continue on my travels." Caleb paused near her, a frown on his face as he watched her. He could see the pain on her face and see the tracks of the tears that she had wept.

"It's okay. I just thought that I was on my own out here. Thank you for stopping." The lady hesitated, assessing Caleb and then deciding that God had provided someone to help her. "My name's Cullea Cassidy. And you would be?"

—

Caleb could hear the faint sound of an accent in her voice. He frowned once more, not recognizing it.

"My name's Caleb Campion. You're in pain." Caleb's words were a statement, not a question.

"I am. I seem to have hurt my ankle somehow." Cullea pointed to the leg that she had extended. "It's hard to put any weight on it."

Caleb shrugged out of his backpack and was on his knees beside her before she had finished speaking. He felt along the leg and ankle, trying to assess how serious the injury was. Cullea gave a whimper and then tried to draw her foot back from Caleb's hands. As gentle as his fingers were, it still hurt.

"It looks as if you have a good sprain here. This just happened?" Caleb looked up when she didn't answer, a frown covering his face for a moment. "Cullea? When did this happen?"

"Last night. I slipped on some loose rocks a ways back on the trail." She didn't look at him, not wanting to see pity on his face. "I managed to make it this far. I was praying that I could make it to the parking lot that I know is just down the trail and maybe find someone to help me."

"Where's your car?" Caleb sat back on his heels, his hand still cradling her foot, his eyes on her face.

"I don't have it here. I was dropped off a ways up the trail two days ago. I was to call for a ride when I reached here last night. Only my phone died and I have no way to call anyone." Cullea drew in a breath, not realizing it was almost a sob.

"Your phone died? Here, you can use mine." Caleb tried to hand over his phone but Cullea kept shaking her head. "Who do you want to call?"

"I don't know. The person who was to give me a ride was leaving town late last night. So I don't know who I can call."

"I'll help you. I wasn't up to anything today." Caleb was on his feet, hearing a sound from the trail. He turned that way, finding himself facing three men, all of whom had weapons pointed at them. His hands rose in the air as he stepped back to stand in front of Cullea. He would protect her as much as he could, Caleb decided.

The men simply watched them and then motioned them to move. Caleb reached to help Cullea to her feet, an arm wrapped around her to help her balance.

"What do you want?" Caleb didn't back down from the men, watching them carefully.

"You're coming with us." The taller of the men motioned with his weapon.

Caleb studied the man and then the other two before he looked down at Cullea. Her head of bright golden hair just reached his shoulder. He sighed. There was no way that Cullea would be able to walk on that ankle. And he just didn't understand who the men were and what they wanted with them. He simply reached to shoulder his backpack and draped Cullea's over his other shoulder. He then gathered her into his arms. Cullea gave a small squeak, her arms tightened around his neck.

Forced back to the main trail, Caleb felt the jab of the weapon in his back. He walked forward on the trail, careful to set his feet down on the trail so that he didn't trip or fall and injure Cullea further.

Three hours later, Caleb felt a tug on the back of his shirt. He stopped, breathing harder than he normally would. His eyes dropped to Cullea, seeing by the look on her face that the pain had increased. He waited for the men to confer before they were once more shoved forward and towards a cabin that sat off to the side of the trail. He didn't recognize it. His senses were alert, knowing that they were in danger. Caleb set Cullea down gently on a chair and then stood behind her, his hands on her shoulders. His eyes were alert and watchful, seeing one of the men standing with his back to the door. The other two men had not entered.

Lord, what have we gotten ourselves into? I don't know who these men are, but I sense that they mean us harm. I want to get Cullea out of here but I'm not sure how or when. Protect us, please, dear Lord. Defend us.

—

Chapter 2

Not moving from behind Cullea, Caleb felt her body shaking with fear. His hands tightened on her shoulders and one of her hands reached up to grasp his. His eyes never moved from the man standing in front of the door. He had glanced briefly around the cabin, a frown on his face. Caleb didn't know the men and had no idea why they had been abducted as they had been.

The man moved away from the door as he heard a slight tap at it. He cracked it open and then spoke quietly with the man who had approached it. He shot a look back at Caleb and Cullea and then stepped from the cabin. The door closed behind him.

Caleb waited, not sure if the man was returning or not. He didn't move, his hands still on Cullea's shoulders before he crouched down beside her. His arm was around her shoulders. Cullea leaned against him, drawing from his strength. She didn't know him but she trusted him. And for her to trust someone that quickly was unusual.

"Cullea? How's your ankle?" Caleb kept his voice low, his eyes shifting between watching her face and watching the door.

"It hurts, if you must know. I need to leave here." Cullea tried to stand, sinking back as she put her foot on the floor and felt the pain radiating up her leg. Tears clouded her eyes for a moment. "I don't cry." She swiped at her face, ashamed that she was weeping.

English, not one another.

Getting down on his knee in front of Lachlan, Robert placed his sword down before him as well and nodded once. "Red Harlaw was a disgrace. We all have suffered too much loss. The Irvines wish to move forward peaceably."

Putting his arm out, Lachlan waited for Robert to do the same and the men clasped wrists in a show of unity before exchanging swords and getting back up on their feet. Sheathing the sword that had killed his brother at Harlaw, Robert felt a chill run up his spine and closed his eyes, remembering the horror of that day, the sight of his brother's blood spilling from his body and staining the green fields red. It would never leave his mind. But life moved forward and, as laird, it was Robert's duty to make certain it did.

"As long as ye hold my father's sword, ye can be certain that the Macleans are allies of the Irvines," Lachlan said slowly as he sheathed Robert's sword. "I dinnae wish to be run through by my father's own sword and I ken ye dinnae wish to be run through by yers, so we shall forever ken there is peace."

"Aye," Robert replied and breathed deeply, hearing Reginald and William stepping forward to flank him in solidarity, knowing he had made the right decision for his people. Reginald smacked him on the back and Robert looked at his brother, nodding in understanding. Alexander died in a battle that should never have happened, led by greedy men with selfish desires. Hopefully, with Robert leading the way, such events would be avoided in the future. Nay, war was always inevitable, but should it occur, Robert prayed there was solidarity amongst his fellow Scots, never against them in vain.

"Ye have traveled far to be here," Robert said to Lachlan, looking at his score of men behind him, all wrapped in plaids and covered in filth.

"Nay journey is too far if it is in the name of peace," Lachlan added. "The Donald is a madman. He will continue to cause trouble in the Highlands, mark my words. My father was little

"It's okay, Cullea. It's okay, sweetheart." Caleb kept his voice low. He reached cautiously for his phone and studied it. He had cell reception. He sent off a quick message to his team leader, Don, knowing that Don would reach out to him, just stating what had happened and where they were. Don would gather his team and some of their friends if needed and head for him. He just didn't know if they would reach them before they were moved again.

Dusk fell quickly in the cabin, the daylight fading outside. Caleb had moved to sit cross-legged on the floor, Cullea's injured foot on his leg. His hand rested on it even as he watched the door. He was patient as he did so, knowing that he could not take on three men by himself.

Cullea wondered at how quiet and still he was. She had shifted many times on her chair, discomfort and pain driving her to do that but also the uncertainty of what they had faced doing that. She had opened her mouth to speak but snapped it closed as Caleb shook his head, a finger to his lips. She nodded. *God, where are You? Are You here? How do we get away? I know that You are in control. It just doesn't seem that way.*

"Caleb? Where are they?" Cullea kept her voice low, not sure if the men were just outside of the door and could hear them.

"Outside, I think. I don't want to open the door unless I am sure that we are on our own." Caleb tilted his head to study her. "I wish I could get you out of here. It's been hours now."

"It has been. You had plans that I'm keeping you from." Cullea sniffed, trying hard not to weep again.

"It's okay, sweetheart. I had no real plans until I met you. Now, I need to keep you safe." Caleb kept his voice low as well. "Just so you know, I work for a security team. I was able to get a text off to the leader of our team about what happened and where we are. He'll gather up some friends and come and find us."

"If we're still here. What if they move us?" Cullea's brow wrinkled as she tried to think of how she could get them free. Only, she couldn't think of any way. She had never been in that kind of situation before.

"We'll figure it out." Caleb set her foot carefully on the floor and rose, walking around the room, listening at the door to see if he could hear the men. He couldn't but he still didn't try the door. God had not given him permission to do that. Instead, it was impressed upon him that they needed to stay right where they were. If they tried to escape, Caleb knew that they would be injured.

He sat back down beside Cullea, reaching to raise her foot once more. He needed to assess it better but he refused to remove her hiking boot. It was helping to provide stability to it. This is when Caleb wished that Thomas, their team paramedic, was there.

"Cullea, have you ever seen these men before?" Caleb waited patiently for her to speak, knowing that she was mulling his question over and over.

"Not that I know of. But then, I don't know many young people. I usually work with seniors or

—

those who are near seniors. I'm an audiologist." Cullea had never volunteered that much information about herself so quickly. She just felt that she could trust Caleb. God had provided that peace to her and she had learned to listen to His leading with people.

"You do? That's an interesting occupation." Caleb frowned for a moment, hearing a sound outside. "Cullea, I will do everything that I can to keep you safe."

"I know that you will, but it may be taken out of your hand. I just don't get it." Cullea's eyes closed for a moment. The pain and fatigue from not sleeping the night before were weighing down her eyes. All she wanted to do was to curl up in a corner somewhere and sleep.

"Don't go to sleep on me, Cullea. I need you to stay awake." Caleb reached for his backpack and pulled out two bottles of water. "Here. Drink some of this. I have food as well if you want something to eat."

Cullea nodded, her eyes cracking open. She took the bottle of water and sipped from it, not sure if she really felt like eating.

"How long will it take for someone to come?" Cullea didn't think that Caleb would be able to answer that question or not.

"I'm not sure, Cullea. It depends on how they come. If Don could find a helicopter to come in and land near here, it wouldn't be too long. They might also find some ATVs to come. I can't tell you how long. I do know that they will come as soon as they can."

As the door opened once more, Caleb was on his feet, his hands clenching into fists and down at his side. He sighed. The three men were back and it didn't look good for Cullea and himself at all.

"On your feet. We're moving." The first man shoved at Caleb, sending him sideways as he was knocked off balance. "Move and now!"

The couple could hear the anger in the man's voice. Caleb reached to gather Cullea into his arms once more, knowing that they were walking again and she just couldn't do it. He just prayed that Don would be able to follow them. He looked down at their backpacks. They would not be able to take them, that much was clear.

Walking through the door, Caleb felt Cullea's arms around his neck. He sighed to himself. He had no idea who these men were or where they were heading. *Lord, I don't know what to do. I can't run and leave Cullea on her own. She's in my care right now. Please, dear Lord, keep us safe. Send Don and my team to find us as soon as they can.*

Chapter 3

Don crept towards the cabin. He had managed to find a friend whose helicopter was free and who had been willing to fly them to near where the cabin sat. Paul, Thomas, Mark, and Joshua, the other team members, crept just as silently as he did. Aidan, a police detective and friend of the men, stood and watched the cabin for a moment before he too moved forward. He had not said "no" when Don had reached out to him, a day off from work or not. He had a bad feeling about this, just as he had with Paul and Thomas when they had been in danger.

His hand touching the door, Don's head tilted for a moment as he listened. He could not hear anything from the cabin and that puzzled him. Caleb should be there as should the lady who he had mentioned. The door opened with a squeak under his hand and all the men winced at the noise.

Standing in the cabin, they stared around and then at one another. Caleb and Cullea were not there and they should have been. It had only been a couple of hours since Don received Caleb's text and with him saying that the lady had an injured ankle, they would not have just walked away.

Mark reached for the backpacks, recognizing Caleb's distinct one. Caleb had purchased it from a friend's son who had decorated it for him. It was not something that he would have left behind, not if he had had any choice in the matter.

"This is Caleb's." Mark held it up. He searched the smaller pack, finding Cullea's name on it. "And this is for a Cullea, Is she the lady with him?"

"More than likely." Joshua reached for it and studied it in turn. "But where are they?"

Aidan walked back outside and around the cabin, studying the footprints. There were at least four that he could distinguish. He sighed to himself, something that he decided he had been doing too much of lately. This was not good, he decided. Caleb and this lady who was named Cullea were captives. He just didn't see any footprints that belonged to a lady. He frowned once more.

"Don?" He turned as Don approached him. "This lady who Caleb mentioned?"

"Cullea? I think that is what he called her. What about her?" Don was somewhat puzzled as to the question. He stared around as well, seeing the underbrush creeping close to the cabin and listening to the sounds of nature that filled his ears. He raised a hand to block the sun for a moment.

"I don't see her footprints. You're sure that there was a lady here?"

"I am. Caleb mentioned that her ankle had been injured. I would suspect that he has been carrying her."

"That would make sense. This doesn't make sense, though. Caleb doesn't make enemies. He collects people. All of your guys do."

Don laughed at that. Aidan had described them all so well.

"And so do you." Don stepped to one side, studying the trail. "I can recognize Caleb's prints. He has a boot with a distinct tread. And it is heavier than his usual print."

The other four men had approached and in turn watched the area around them. They did not sense any danger at the present but their thoughts and prayers were with their team mate. Was he undergoing an adventure now? They prayed that he wasn't but they were certain that he was.

"That must mean that Caleb is carrying her." Paul spoke up. "He would not let her walk on an injured foot."

"No, he wouldn't. None of us would." Joshua echoed that sentiment. "Now what, Don?"

"We can't do much right now. It will be dark soon and Kaelen needs to head back." Don turned to stare behind him. "So, how do we do this? We're not prepared to be out here for long."

"We head back home and come back tomorrow better prepared to track them. Sunday and all? We need to do this?" Aidan pointed towards the path. "Let's head off and then come back early in the morning. Kaelen said that he was available."

None of the men wanted to leave without finding their team mate. They knew that he was in danger, just given the circumstances. Yet, they had to leave. They were not prepared to be out there overnight. When they returned in the morning, they would be prepared to search. All they could do is pray for Caleb.

Kaelen watched his friends returning, not seeing Caleb with them. He hadn't been found then, he decided. That meant they would want to return in the morning. And this time he would bring them and then do some searching from the air. Caleb was a good friend who had shared many a meal with him and spent many hours in prayer and Bible study.

Don paced his home that night. He was deeply worried about Caleb. He had prayed that none of the rest of the team would undergo what Paul and Thomas had. It seems as if Caleb was now on an adventure of his own.

The team met before the sun had even risen the next morning. Aidan and Kaelen had simply appeared with the others, meeting for prayer before they made plans.

Kaelen ferried the men in two groups to an area near where they had found the cabin the day before. He watched as they walked away, intent on finding Caleb that morning. He shifted on his seat and then sighed. The helicopter lifted off as Kaelen flew around the area, searching himself for any signs of Caleb and the lady that seemed to be with him. He found nothing. Searching further, he frowned. There was that other cabin, the location that he had been trying to remember. He set the helicopter down in a nearby clearing and reached for his phone.

Don pulled out his phone, frowning. Why was Kaelen calling him?

"Don? I found another cabin. It would be a couple of hours' walk from where you are. I'm on the ground and heading in." Kaelen didn't wait for Don to respond, simply ending the call and heading out.

Don gave a frustrated sound, turning to the men who had stopped walking as he took a call.

"Don? What happened?" Aidan waited for him to speak.

"Kaelen. He's found another cabin a couple of hours from here. He's going in to look." Don didn't want him to do that, knowing that he could be walking into danger.

The men shared looks and then turned to the path. They had found the evidence again from last night that Caleb had been walked away from the cabin. Heading out, their eyes and senses were alert all the while they prayed for God to protect their friend.

Chapter 4

Standing in the shadows of the trees that surrounded the cabin, Kaelen waited. He wasn't sure if he should move towards the cabin or wait. He finally walked carefully towards the cabin or hut or whatever someone wanted to call it. It wasn't in great shape, he decided. Kaelen's hand touched the door, finding it swinging open. That startled him and he hesitated before he shoved it open all the way.

Dust motes flew around as he entered. Kaelen waved his hand to clear the dust motes away from his vision. Hearing a slight sound, he spun, his gaze landing on a lady who was sitting nearby, her hands covering her mouth. His eyes dropped to search the floor before he gave an explanation and sprang towards Caleb.

Unconscious, Caleb had not been able to try and release his wrists. They had been bound behind him. Cullea had tried to undo the knot but that had not worked out so well. The man who had bound him the night before had made sure that the knot would not be able to be untied.

The men had walked Caleb towards the cabin. He was growing fatigued, walking without a break and carrying Cullea. But he would not say anything. Cullea was not able to walk on her own and Caleb would not even ask her to try. He admired the character that she was showing. He knew that it was awkward for her and that she was in pain but she didn't grumble or say a word.

—

Shoved towards the cabin at last and into it, Caleb had set Cullea gently on the dirt floor, helping her to lean against one of the walls of the ramshackle hut that he decided it was. He stood upright, his height dwarfing the men in front of him to some degree. He watched them closely, standing in front of Cullea. Caleb had no idea what they wanted from them or which one had been the actual target. That had not been made clear. The men had not spoken to them at all. When they had a conversation among themselves, they walked away to do so.

The men spread out around Caleb and he was unable to watch all of them. He heard Cullea scream and then a hard blow on the back of his head. Caleb fell forward, his body hitting hard on the dirt. He didn't move. Cullea stared at him in horror before her eyes raised to stare at the men. She shuddered at the cold, hard looks that were directed her way. One of the men knelt beside Caleb, roughly dragging his arms behind his back. A rope was handed to him and then the man wrapped it around Caleb's wrists. He rose, his eyes on Cullea before the three men turned and walked away.

Cullea struggled to crawl towards Caleb, sobs shaking her body. She was overtired, hurting, and in despair. Her hands had reached out to Caleb, touching his face and feeling to see if he was really still alive. Her hand found the lump on the back of his head. There was no blood but it was large.

Dusk fell not long after that. Cullea remained where she was, a hand resting on Caleb's back, feeling it rise and fall with his breathing. She wrapped her other arm around herself to try and keep warm. That just didn't seem to happen. Finally, she looked around and then laid down close to Caleb, an arm around him. She slept at some point, waking every little while. The sounds of the critters in the shack and outside disturbed her. Cullea was afraid, more afraid than she had ever been. She prayed for protection for them both and for dawn to come quickly. She also begged God for Caleb to rouse. That didn't seem to be happening. She needed him to wake up.

A few hours after the sun rose, Cullea looked up as the door moved. She screamed as a man appeared, startling him. The man stared at her before he was across to kneel beside her. Cullea tried to move backwards only to hit Caleb, who had still not moved. That fact had frightened her. She was sure that he was dying and she didn't want that to happen. Cullea was convinced that it was her fault that they had been kidnapped.

"I'm sorry. I didn't mean to scare you." Kaelen watched her closely before he moved around her to kneel beside Caleb. He reached for his pocket knife and made short work of cutting his bonds. "What happened?"

"They knocked him out. I haven't been able to get him to wake up. They did it and then left." Cullea stared down at Caleb even as Kaelen shifted Caleb to his back. "I just know that he's going to die, isn't he? He hasn't woken up since they hit him last night.'

"Last night? You've been alone since last night?" Kaelen continued to try and rouse Caleb to no avail.

"They left in the early evening. I didn't have any water to give him. They just left us here. Was that to die?" Cullea blinked rapidly, hating the tears that just had to gather in her eyes.

"That's okay. I have some in my copter. Are you able to walk at all?" Kaelen studied her for a moment, seeing that she was shaking her head. "You can't?"

"No, I don't think so. I mean, I can try but it would be really slow." Cullea drew in a deep breath. "You need me to, don't you? You won't leave either one of us by ourselves. How far would I need to walk?"

"About fifteen minutes." Kaelen was on his feet, drawing Caleb to his feet and then over his shoulders. He then extended a hand to Cullea, helping her to stand. "I'll walk really slow, Cullea, is it? If you hold my hand, we may be able to do that."

Cullea nodded, knowing that it would hurt and hurt really badly but she was determined to do her best to walk. Kaelen nodded to himself. He would do what he could to get her to the copter and then to help.

Twenty minutes later, Cullea leaned against the copter, the toes of her injured foot touching the ground. She was in severe pain and the tears were near the surface. She was praying hard for Caleb and not for herself. She didn't care about that. Cullea just wanted Caleb to be well.

Kaelen shifted Caleb to a seat and buckled him in. He then turned to Cullea, gathering her into his arms and doing the same for her. Cullea gave a small squeak as he did so.

Kaelen pulled out his phone, hesitating for a moment before he dialled a number.

"Don? Where are you?" Kaelen waited patiently for Don to figure that out.

"About twenty minutes from the original cabin. Why?" Don held up a hand stopping the group with him.

"I have Caleb and Cullea. Cullea is injured. I'm not sure if it's just a sprain of her ankle or if it's broken. Caleb was knocked out yesterday and is still out. Head back for the cabin. I'll head for town and then come back for you."

"Take care of them. We'll head back for the parking lot. Have someone meet us there." Don pocketed his phone, turning to the group. "Good news. Kaelen had found them and is heading in with them. Caleb is unconscious. Cullea is hurt as well. We'll get all the particulars when we meet up with them."

Aidan had listened carefully before he walked away. His phone was out as he called in to the police department, asking that someone meet Kaelen at the airport and then help transport Caleb and Cullea to the hospital. He also asked that a patrol officer stayed with each of the couple until he arrived.

The group turned, walking rapidly away from that spot and towards the parking lot. They knew that someone would be there to meet them. Kaelen would have arranged for that. Don's phone was out once more, calling for help. He didn't want to wait if he could help it. He was that worried about Caleb.

Each of the men prayed for their friend and team mate. They weren't sure how badly he was hurt and that worried them. They had shared a look when Don had spoken, knowing that he was worried as well.

—

Chapter 5

Walking into the hospital, Don looked around, searching for Kaelen. He found him waiting near the door to the examination rooms in the Emergency Department. He pointed towards seats and Don moved that way.

"Kaelen? What is the word?" Don watched his team members gather around them.

"He was starting to rouse somewhat by the time that I landed. They're both being assessed right now. They know that you were on your way in. Caleb's family?"

"His parents are out of town for a couple of months. They're with a short-term mission and are difficult to reach." Don sighed, knowing that if Caleb was hurt seriously that he would do his best to contact them. He just didn't know how to do that.

"That's right. I had forgotten that they were gone." Kaelen hesitated for a moment. "The lady with Caleb? Cullea? What's the story there?"

"I have no idea. I don't know anyone by that name." Don watched as Aidan walked towards the doors and into the restricted area. "Aidan will find out for us. If she's in danger, Caleb won't walk away from her and neither will any of us."

"No, we won't." Kaelen was on his feet. "Sorry, Don. I need to run. I just call a call to head out on a search and rescue."

"Go on, Kaelen. Call me when you get back. I might have more information at that point." Don watched him walk away before he was back on his feet, gathering his team around him. "We don't know anything yet."

"Okay. So, what do we do? In the meantime, we don't have enough information to start searching." Mark was thinking through what to do.

"No, we don't. Until we speak with Caleb and then the lady, we won't know what is going on." Joshua paced away and back to his friends. "We don't know the lady's name other than her first name. And I don't recognize it."

"I don't know that any of us do." Paul rubbed at his face and then turned as he felt a hand on his back. His wife, Payten, was there as was Thomas' wife, Taran. Both men wrapped an arm around their wives. "Payten? You're here?"

"I am. Kaelen called me and I called Taran. You need us here. I hear that there is a lady involved?" Payten frowned. As far as she knew, Caleb was not dating. "Who is she?"

"We don't know, sweetheart." Paul watched as a physician exited the exam room area and headed for Don. "Don? There's the doc."

Don looked around the men and then headed for the physician. He disappeared behind the doors with him.

Paul sighed even as his arm tightened around Payten. They had all prayed that the adventures as they had called them ended with Thomas. This doesn't seem to be happening. The men found seats, their heads bowing as they petitioned God for their friend and the lady who was with him.

Don paused beside Caleb's stretcher, a prayer rising from him as well. He knew that God was in control and had allowed this. He rested a hand on the bedrail, watching as Caleb gradually regained consciousness.

Caleb stared around, his eyes narrowed as he stared at the room. A hospital room? What did he go and do? His head turned as he found Don standing there, a concerned look on his face.

"Caleb? How's the head?" Don winced as Caleb moved and his eyes slid closed against the pain.

"It hurts. What did I do?" Caleb was having trouble with his memory. Something was niggling at the edge of it, someone whom he knew was in danger. He just couldn't remember.

"You went and got yourself hit over the head." Don turned as he heard soft thumps on the floor. A beautiful lady appeared in the doorway, balancing somewhat unsteadily on crutches.

Caleb looked around Don, frowning at the lady. He felt that he should know her. Only he couldn't remember her.

Don walked over to her, a hand out to help her.

"You must be Cullea. Caleb is awake and somewhat in his right mind. Are you okay?" Don grinned at her.

Cullea looked up at him, somewhat in shock at how he spoke. Her eyes then went to Caleb before she thumped her way across the floor to stand and stare at him. She was puzzled. He was looking at her as if he really didn't know her.

"Caleb? Are you okay?" Her voice was quiet, almost as if she didn't think that she should ask him.

"I am, I think. I'm sorry. I know that we've met. I just can't remember it." Caleb reached to raise the head of his bed, his eyes closing as he fought the vertigo that ensued. His eyes opened to see the horrified look on Cullea's face.

"You shouldn't have done that." Cullea was so afraid that he was hurt worse than she thought. "I'm Cullea. You came to my assistance yesterday morning and then we were abducted. We were left in a shack overnight. You were knocked out. A friend of yours found us this morning."

Caleb reached for her hand, stilling the restless movement of it on the crutch. She stared at his hand holding hers and then at him. She frowned, not sure what to think. Caleb looked past her to Don, who was simply shaking his head at him and trying his best to hide his smile.

"Cullea? Did they hurt you, whoever they were?" Caleb was greatly worried about her.

"No. They did you. They hit you and then tied you up. Then they just walked away. A friend of yours showed up this morning with his helicopter and brought us here." Cullea slumped on her crutches, fatigue wearing on her. "Where are we?"

"In my town, Cullea. Don? I'm allowed to leave?" Caleb tilted his head to stare past the beautiful lady whose hand he was holding and who he was deeply afraid would walk away from him. He refused to acknowledge or at the very least didn't realize that she had already walked into his heart and taken it over.

"I don't know what town that is, though." Cullea's face crumpled for a moment as tears tracked down her face.

Caleb muttered something and then was sitting on the side of the stretched and wrapping her into his arms. His head pounded at the sudden movement, causing his own face to show his pain.

Don once more shook his head, turning as he heard footsteps. The physician stood there with their discharge papers.

"Don? Where are they heading? Caleb shouldn't be on his own tonight."

"To my place. Daci's heading that way, she said. Cullea? Let's get you out of here and to my home. My sister will meet us there. And yes, you can bring Caleb with you." Don simply grinned at the glare that Caleb sent his way.

Chapter 6

Caleb's feet hit the tiled floor in the examination room, his hand resting on Cullea's arm. He frowned as he saw how she was hesitating before he turned her towards the door. Don watched his care of her with slight amusement before he was stopping Caleb.

"Caleb, let me have your keys. One of the guys will pick up your truck and bring it my way. They'll stop at your place and pick up some clean clothes for you. You're staying with me tonight." Don's eyes strayed to Cullea, seeing the distress on her face. "Cullea, you're with us. My sister will meet us at my place. She'll have done some shopping for you as well, knowing Daci. And we did recover your backpacks from the first cabin."

Thomas reached for Caleb's keys, assessing the couple before he and Joshua walked away, heading for the parking lot and then to find Caleb's truck. The two ladies studied Cullea before they moved in on her, startling her.

"Hi. I'm Payten. I'm married to one of Caleb's friend, Paul. This is Taran. She's married to Thomas. We'll meet you at Don's."

Cullea stared at them before she blinked rapidly. *God? Is this You? Did You provide these ladies for me today? I haven't had a lot of friends over the years. And I need that. You know how many times I have cried to you about this. Thank You.*

Cullea nodded, a shy smile on her face.

———

"Thank you. I'm Cullea Cassidy. Don't ask me the history of what happened. I don't know." She stared in surprise at the ladies as they began to laugh.

"It's okay, Cullea." Taran spoke up, knowing that they had confused the lady in front of them. "We both had life and death adventures with our guys. It looks as if you're off on one of your own."

"Oh, no, I'm not. I don't have a guy. I never will." A sad look crossed her face, causing Caleb to drape an arm across her shoulder. She jumped as she felt that.

"It's okay, Cullea. We'll figure it out." Caleb looked around, feeling as if they were being watched. "How be we head out of here?"

Don agreed. He too had a feeling that there were onlookers there that meant Caleb and Cullea harm.

Daci watched as Caleb walked towards the house, keeping step with the lady on crutches. She sighed to herself. *Caleb is in the middle of this now, isn't he, Lord? How do we keep him safe and solve this before they come to harm?*

Cullea stared at the house and then at the lady waiting for her. Her steps stopped and she hesitated, not sure if she was really welcome. She knew that Caleb was beside her. She felt his arm across her shoulders and then headed his prayer for her. Cullea felt relieved that she seemed to have landed among believers. Her parents would have been grateful for that. Needing her mother and not having her was not easy. And she had no way to reach out to them. They were deep in a country where communications were spotty at best.

Daci's eyes raised to Don who shook his head. There were questions that they all had and he doubted that Caleb or Cullea would hav the answers that they were all searching for either. He could hear the footsteps of the others behind him. Daci would have prepared a meal for them but he doubted that either Caleb or Cullea would want to eat before they cleaned up. At least, that's what he would want and he was confident that Caleb would feel the same way.

Showered, her hair washed, and dressed in clean clothes, Cullea hesitated before she reached for the door knob. Once she opened it, she knew that she would be facing questions, questions that she had no answer for. Just how did Caleb come to be there, she questioned once more. She knew that he had planned to walk the trail and camp out overnight. Only she didn't know how he had planned that. Meeting her and then being abducted had changed it all.

Caleb looked up, wincing at the pain in his head, as the door in front of him opened. He had cleaned up himself and had stood, leaning against the wall across from the door, patiently waiting for Cullea to appear. Once the door opened, he studied her and then moved in on her, simply wrapping her into a hug. It startled her before she balanced her crutches against her body and hugged him back. She missed her parents' hug. Her family was a hugging family.

"Okay, sweetheart?" Caleb's voice was low, just loud enough for her to hear.

Cullea frowned against him as she heard the word of endearment. She thought that he had made a mistake when he said that. No man would ever be calling her that, she was convinced.

"I think so. The ankle feels better now that it's strapped. I just don't understand any of this."

"It's okay. Tonight, we'll share a meal with my friends, tell them what we know and then plan on working on it tomorrow. We take tonight to rest and recover." Caleb turned her towards the large kitchen that at the moment seemed to be overrun with people. He knew that both Aidan and Kaelen had appeared, willing to share a meal +with their friends.

Cullea was quiet as they shared their meal. Daci kept studying her, knowing that she likely felt out of place among the friends. She turned her gaze to Caleb, finding that man watching Cullea as well, a look on his face that she had seen on the faces of two others of her brother's team.

"Don? Aidan? I don't understand this. I was just heading out on a hike overnight when I found Cullea just sitting there. She had managed to get near the parking lot near here. The men appeared and then took us captive. They made us walk to that cabin, waited for a while and then made us walk to the second cabin. I think that's where they knocked me out."

"It was, Caleb." Cullea shifted on her seat*, her ankle starting to ache. The pain medication was wearing off and she just wanted to elevate it. "They knocked you out, tied you up, and then just left. They didn't leave anything with us."

—

Caleb had turned to study her, knowing what she had said. He paled as he realized that with himself unconscious and Cullea injured, it could have turned out a lot worse for them than it had.

Aidan had been listening closely, his note pad out to take the notes that he needed. He knew that the two had given statements at the hospital, although he doubted that Caleb would remember much of that. He rose, excusing himself for a moment as he had to take a call. He stood where he could watch the group in the kitchen. Aidan sensed that Caleb and Cullea were off on their own adventure and that he had prayed would never happen to another one of Don's team.

Chapter 7

Curling up in bed a few hours later, Cullea was unable to pray, overwhelmed with the kindness that had been shown to her. She had not expected it, not at all. She slept at last, knowing that her prayers had been heard.

Caleb shifted on the bed that he had been told to use. He was glad that Don's home had a number of bedrooms. It was not the first time one of the team had used it and he had this deep uneasy feeling that he would not be the last. His prayers were raised as well as he sought to find a comfortable place to lay his head and not doing that. At last, Caleb slept, finding rest where he didn't think that he would.

Don didn't sleep that night. His team was due to train a new security team the next day. Caleb's training on vehicles would just not happen at the beginning of the training as it usually would. He was worried about him but also concerned about Cullea. He reached to wake up his computer and then brought up the programs that he usually used for investigations. Don searched, not finding much about Cullea. That surprised him to some degree but then he shrugged. He rose in the early morning hours, stretching and then heading for the kitchen, his empty coffee mug in hand.

Cullea roused as she heard Don's footsteps. She squinted at the clock and then sighed. She needed to be up and at work. Only she had quit her work as an audiologist that Friday before and walked away from her apartment for the moment. She needed a break that she had not had in many years. She was worn out and exhausted. And she had to acknowledge to herself that she had not felt safe in months in her hometown. She had talked with her father who had not been able to help much other than to warn her to be aware at all times of where she was and who was around her. He had walked away from her that day, disturbed and deeply worried. Cowan had turned in the doorway to watch his daughter, seeing the fear in her and not able to relieve it as he had when she was young.

Don looked around as he heard Cullea's crutches and reached for the teapot to make her tea. He smiled as she hesitated in the doorway.

"Good morning, Cullea. Did you get any sleep?" He simply pointed to a chair.

"I did, thank you, Don." Cullea sat, not sure if she should.

"Caleb has not been up yet, not that I know of. He'll sleep a lot in the next couple of days, just trying to recover. How's the ankle?"

"It hurts, if you must know. It's not broken, but it is a bad sprain. I can't weight bear for a number of days." She blinked as he nodded, compassion on his face. "I don't have work to get to, which is a blessing."

Don looked up as he heard Caleb's footsteps, sending him a nod to sit beside Cullea. Cullea looked up as she felt his arm around her, a frown on her face that he kept doing that. She didn't allow men to do that other than her father.

Caleb nodded as Don held up the coffee pot. He needed one that morning, feeling even worse than he had the night before. His eyes were on Cullea as she sat quietly, her hands wrapped around her own mug. He could hear Don and Daci speaking quietly before a meal was set in front of them. He tilted his head further to study her, fear for her in his heart and mind. He needed to determine who the men were. He had not recognized them. Caleb had given the description to Aidan but he didn't know if Aidan would be able to help much.

Daci rose at last, drawing Cullea with her. Cullea was reluctant to leave Caleb, feeling safe with him. Caleb had risen to his feet, watching as she left. He heard Don stop beside him, his hand resting on his shoulder.

"Caleb? What do we do with Cullea? She has to have a home and family." Don turned his head as he heard the back door open and nodded at the other four men who had entered. It was still early enough that the new team had not yet appeared. He knew that they would within the hour.

"I'm not sure where she's from or what is going on with her. We didn't talk at all. I was too busy watching out for her and watching the men. Then I was knocked out and we couldn't. We do need to talk with her but we have our team in for training." Caleb swayed on his feet, his headache beating at his temples in a violent manner.

Thomas, the paramedic on the team, reached to steady him. He then shoved him gently towards the living room, knowing that Caleb needed to be off his feet. Caleb sank onto the couch, nodding slightly. Thomas simply handed him an ice pack.

"Lie down, Caleb. You're not teaching today, not at this rate. Put the ice pack on the back of your neck. It will help." Thomas watched with sympathy and compassion as Caleb did that, a sigh coming from the other man as the ice pack hit the back of his neck.

Daci had appeared, a question on her lips for Caleb. Seeing him on the couch, she hesitated and then turned back to where Cullea was huddled on a couch in the office. She was conflicted, not sure what to do. Joshua followed her, his hand out to stop her in the hallway.

"Daci? What was it that you wanted from Caleb?" Joshua waited patiently for her to speak.

"I just needed him to be with Cullea. I can't reach through to her. Caleb seems to be the only one who can." Daci held out a piece of paper. "She did tell me where she lives and what she does for work. She also gave me her parents' names but said that they were away on a mission trip and were very difficult to reach."

Joshua took the piece of paper, his eyes on Cullea. She had raised her head and was watching him, a shuttered look on her face. He sighed to himself. This was going to be difficult. None of them had spent enough time speaking with her to establish any sort of relationship. Caleb had done that with how he had tried to protect him. Joshua didn't need to know the details to know that was what he had done.

—

"We'll look into it, Daci." Joshua walked away, pausing in the living room to study his team mate. Caleb had dozed off, he could tell. He turned then and walked out of the house and towards the office building. He found his office, sat, and pulled up the programs that he needed to. Mark found him, sitting across the desk from him.

"What's going on, Joshua?" Neither man was due for training that morning and had time to investigate Cullea.

"Daci found some information on Cullea. Caleb's not up to investigating so I thought that I would."

Chapter 8

Cullea finally found a seat in the living room, her eyes on Caleb. She wanted him awake but knew that he had to sleep to heal. Daci had moved away from her, heading for the kitchen with an eye on the clock. The men would be in soon for a meal and she was needing to prepare something. She hesitated for a moment, her phone out to send a text message to both Payten and Taran. Cullea needed more clothes until they could get her back to her own him. The two ladies responded that they had already thought of that and were shopping for her. Did Daci know what she needed?

Cullea looked around as Daci sat near her. A frown covered her face for a moment. She sighed. She needed to find a way home but didn't know who to ask. She wasn't sure enough of the men here to ask that of them. Caleb was the only one that she would and he was not capable of driving at the moment.

Aidan paused in the doorway. He had returned to speak with both Caleb and Cullea. He shook his head as he saw Caleb asleep. Aidan turned to Cullea, finding her watching him in turn. He nodded.

"Cullea? How are you today?" Aidan found a seat near her, taking with thanks the mug of coffee that Daci handed him. He could hear soft conversation in the kitchen and knew that the other ladies were there.

"I have no idea how I'm to feel. Do you?" Cullea's eyes closed. That question was not her. "I'm sorry. I didn't mean that."

"It's okay, Cullea. It's natural to feel that way. What can we do for you?" Aidan waited patiently for her to think that through.

"I need to go home. I can't stay here." Cullea's face fell as she looked down. She felt ashamed that she was in the position that she was.

"It's okay to feel that way too, Cullea. Victims of crime do feel that way." He nodded as her head shot up. "You are a victim of crime, Cullea. God was with you and protected you when you were a captive. He is here with you now. If you really want to go home, we'll get you there. But I don't think that you do. I think that you were running when you took off to walk the Bruce Trail."

Cullea finally nodded. Aidan was correct. She had been running and had not wanted to acknowledge that. Cullea had been wanting to move for years and maybe even change her occupation. She felt trapped at home, even though she wasn't. She just couldn't explain her feelings that well.

"No, I don't know that I want to go back there. I quit my job last week and was thinking of moving somewhere else. Mom and Dad are away for at least six to seven months of the year on short-term missions or conferences. They wouldn't want me to stay in my hometown just for them. I guess that I was hiking just to think it through. I slid on some loose rocks and that's when I hurt my ankle. I had managed to walk forward, praying that I would find someone. Caleb found me and then those men did. Who were they?"

—

"We don't know, Cullea. We don't have enough information on them to know that. All we can do is continue to search through the records and see if we find anyone who matches one of them. In the meantime, we need you to be as careful as you can. When you are out and about, be with someone. Be aware of your surroundings. I know the three ladies here would be willing to do that. If not them, we have others who will. I have had police officers volunteer to do that on their off time."

"They can't do that!" Cullea was horrified at the thought. "They don't know me."

"No, you are correct when you say that. However, they know Don and his team. Don's security team has helped out many people without asking for anything in return. He has friends who will help as well." Aidan was adamant about that. He watched as Caleb roused and then sat up, rubbing at his temples while watching Cullea. "Caleb? Is that not correct?"

Cullea's head shot around as Aidan spoke to Caleb. She realized that he was indeed awake once more.

"Aidan's right, Cullea. We will protect you as much as we can. I know that Daci will have you stay with her. She's done that before." Caleb could see Daci nodding. "If you need to go back to your hometown for any reason, we'll make it work."

Cullea was at a loss for words, not that she said much anyway. She was quiet, not speaking a lot to others. She nodded at last, knowing that she was being taken care of in a way that only her parents could and would.

"I need my Mom." Tears clouded her eyes for a moment.

"Let me have the details, Cullea. I'll speak to the mission and see what we can do. We have a friend or two who would gladly fly into where they are and bring them out. Not Kaelen. He doesn't fly planes." Aidan grinned at her, hearing Kaelen's voice in the kitchen. He had appeared, Aidan knew, just to assess the couple in front of them. He frowned for a moment before he nodded. Aidan saw the look in Caleb's eyes. He's found his lady in danger, just as Paul and Thomas did.

Lord, please protect my friend and his lady. They are in danger and we have no idea from whom or why. But You do. You are in control. Help us to remember that as we work to solve this. And solve it we will.

Kaelen appeared in the living room, a grin on his face as Cullea stared at him before she frowned.

"Are you supposed to be flying somewhere?" Her voice sounded somewhat disgruntled.

Kaelen laughed even as Caleb and Aidan grinned.

"No at the moment. I'm done for the day. And how are you this fine day?" Kaelen's smile widened at the look on Cullea's face.

"I have no idea how to feel. Isn't that what they all say?" Cullea sighed, opened her mouth to apologize, and then snapped it closed as Kaelen shook his head.

"It's okay, Cullea. It's not the first time someone has responded like that. And it not likely will be the last." Kaelen nodded towards Caleb, seeing that the other man's eyes were somewhat brighter. "Work with Caleb and his team. They'll help solve this. And your parents? Aidan is correct. We do have friends who would fly in today and bring them home."

"They would? They don't know them." Cullea was puzzled at the statement that both Aidan and Kaelen had made.

"It doesn't matter, sweetheart." Caleb reached to pull her down beside him from where she had jumped to her feet, ready to run. "It's what we do and who we are. A friend calls it being the hands and feet of Christ on earth."

Cullea had turned her head to watch him, seeing something in his eyes that caused her to pause.

"That's what Dad always says. Thank you."

—

Chapter 9

Two days later, Caleb walked towards the office building. The headache was easing and he felt ready to work. Don had just looked at him when he appeared in Don's kitchen that morning before shaking his head. Don knew that Caleb was not quite up to working but he would do so just not to let his team down.

Sitting down gratefully in his desk chair, Caleb rested his head in his hands. It had taken more effort to do this than he had bargained for. He raised his head, thinking of Cullea. He had spent some time with the lady last night and was planning on doing the same thing that night. Daci had opened her home up to Cullea until that lady had decided what she wanted to do and where she wanted to live. Somehow, Daci didn't think that Cullea would be leaving their town.

Mark had watched Caleb walking through the building and had followed him, trying hard to assess him. Caleb could be a difficult read when he was sick and that made it difficult in this situation.

Caleb's eyes shifted to watch Mark, hearing the other men laughing and joking with one another in the building. The men from the other team were gathering soon and Caleb knew that he would need to meet them.

"Caleb? Should you be here?" Mark spoke at last, his head turning as he heard footsteps stopping at the doorway. Joshua had appeared and then entered to sit in another chair, his eyes on Caleb as well.

"I have to be, Mark. I'm okay. As long as I don't turn too quickly, the headache isn't too bad. Don is depending on me as are you all." He looked down at the schedule on his desk. "I see that I'm on duty today."

"You are. We'll adjust that depending on how you are feeling."

"I'll get there." He looked back at his friends. "Where do we stand with our investigation so far?"

"Nowhere. There is not enough information to even begin. I spoke with Emma last night. She's starting what she can." Joshua spoke of a friend of theirs who did investigations and found people and information that no one else could. Her husband, Abe, had a security team that now did training as well.

"That's what I thought you would say. Cullea wants to head back to her place this weekend. She's adamant that she's not moving back there. She just wants to pack up everything and close her apartment. I told her that we would go."

"Of course we will. Richard's team will as well. She's content to stay with Daci for now?" Mark was thinking through things, trying to come up with a plan.

"She is. She's worried about Daci being hurt but for now, she's staying there. She's also looking for work here."

"What's her occupation?" Paul spoke from where he stood in the doorway.

"She's an audiologist." Caleb studied his friend, a frown on his face. "Why?"

"I was just wondering. They are looking for an audiologist in the children's department at the hospital. If she's interested, she could apply. It might be a change for her if she's only worked with adults."

"And she had. There's security there too which would help." Caleb sat back before he reached for his phone, sending off a quick text message to Cullea.

Cullea stared at the message, wonder on her face. *God, is this You? Are You the One who had Caleb send this? I have wanted for years to work with children. This may well be the opportunity that I am looking for. I just don't know how safe that I am to do this.*

Daci, with a rare week day off, had sat beside Cullea, her head tilting to watch her face. It had been a text message from Caleb, she decided.

"Cullea? Is something wrong?" Daci's voice broke into Cullea's thoughts.

"No, I don't think so. Caleb just let me know that the hospital is looking for an audiologist to work with children. That's something that I have always wanted to do." Cullea still had a stunned look on her face.

"Well, then, let's look it up." Daci was on her feet, pulling Cullea with her. She shoved the other lady down in her desk chair and pulled up a chair beside her. "Let's pull up the hospital website and see what we need to do. Do you have a resume?"

"I do. I keep my updated on a cloud account. Thank goodness that I do." Cullea quickly pulled up her account. "I can download it to your computer?"

"Of course you can. Now, here's the website. And Caleb was right. Go ahead and apply for it, Cullea. Come find me when you're done." Daci hesitated a moment. "You're not going back to your hometown."

"No, I'm not. Mom and Dad would not hold me there if I wanted to move. And I do. I need to. Something is driving me from there and I don't know what." Cullea looked sad for a moment. "God is there in this but I still feel sad."

"It's normal to feel that way. I see it all the time in my work at the woman's shelter. Now, we need to close out your apartment and move you here. We can put what you don't want to use into a storage unit for now. Don has an empty building that he would let you use. We can round up enough people to help on Saturday. I know that Aidan and Toryn, our police chief and a good friend, would help. Kaelen is very worried about you as well. He'd be there. There are enough to pack you up very quickly. I think that we need to."

Cullea turned to stare at Daci. Daci had just expressed her own thoughts. She felt that she needed to close up that apartment and do it right away. She nodded at Daci before her attention went back to the website and the application that she had found.

Chapter 10

Saturday morning found Cullea tucked between Caleb and Kaelen in the backseat of Don's truck. Daci was in the front seat, her head turning as she watched the traffic around them. The other team members, Aidan, and Toryn had sorted themselves out into vehicles. Cullea had been surprised to see the police chief there even though Daci had maintained that he was a good friend of theirs. She had also been surprised to see how young he was, not much older than herself.

Her hand was tight in Caleb's. She had stared at it for a moment and then at him, finding him just grinning at her. Her crutches were tucked into the bed of the truck, waiting for her to use them once more. She would heartily be glad to be rid of them. Cullea was thanking God for the friends who she had found in Oak City and then too for the work that had appeared. She had been through her interviews and been hired to start in two weeks. She was looking forward to those new duties. Cullea just wished that her parents were there. She needed them.

Caleb was healing rapidly, as he always did. His main concern that day was Cullea and keeping her safe. Don's truck was tucked between other vehicles, the men deciding that needed to be done. He had also arranged for a friend with a moving company to meet them mid-morning at Cullea's apartment. He had promised to do so, bringing the supplies that would be needed.

Cullea sat quietly as Don parked near her apartment. She was happy to be leaving but sad at the same time. She could feel danger approaching her, without warning, and that scared her more than she wanted to admit. Now that the moment had arrived, she was not sure that she wanted to do this.

Caleb's hand tightened on hers, bringing her eyes to him. She could see the compassion and concern on his face before his head bowed and he began to pray for her. She heard the others in the truck following his lead. Her head raised as she stared through the windshield. Cullea was ready to do this as hard as it would be. It was taking her into uncharted territory.

Caleb slid from the truck, reaching to help Cullea out and then reaching for her crutches. His hand on her back gave her the confidence that she needed to move forward.

The group with her mingled around her, protecting her from whoever it was that was near. They could all feel the danger that surrounded both Caleb and Cullea. She paused at the apartment building doorway, seeing the moving truck coming to a stop. Inside, Cullea handed her keys to Don and gave him the apartment number. She headed for the manager's office, Caleb keeping step with her.

The manager was surprised to see Cullea on crutches and was very concerned about her. She was one of his favourite tenants, always willing to help out another but not causing any problems. He listened carefully as she simply stated that she was giving up the apartment and moving to another town. He stated that he would be sad to see her go but wished her all the best. He watched her walk away, studying Caleb as he moved step by step with her.

Three hours later, Cullea balanced on her crutches, leaning into Caleb. He stood with an arm around her, a smile on his face as he listened to the teasing that was going on among his friends. They had just opened up their circle and absorbed Cullea into it. He had been puzzled by the look that Cullea kept shifting to the mail that one of them had retrieved for her.

"Something wrong with the mail, sweetheart?" Caleb's voice was low in her ear.

"There is. There are some envelopes there that only have my name on them. How did they get into a locked mail box?" Cullea was puzzled by that.

Caleb looked around and then beckoned for both Aidan and Toryn to approach them.

"Guys? Cullea has some letters that shouldn't have been in the locked mail box. We'll let you have them." Caleb sorted through the letters and handed the dozen suspicious ones to Aidan.

"I wondered if there were any mail." Aidan took them, looked over the envelopes and then tucked them into a pocket. Toryn watched as well, his eyes turning to Cullea.

"Thank you. Can we leave?" Cullea wanted out of there. Her fear was growing minute by minute.

—

"We can. Hey, everyone? We're ready to go. Don? We're meeting back at your place?" Caleb raised his voice, catching everyone's attention.

"We are. Before we leave, Cullea, we would like to pray with you as you start a new adventure." Don was as good as his word, followed by all of the friends.

Cullea slid onto the truck seat, finding Kaelen on one side again and Caleb on the other. She was grateful for the support of her new friends. She had not expected them all to show up but they had. Someone named Richard had also shown up, stayed for a while, hugged her, prayed for her, and then left. She had stared at him until Mark had laughed and said that Don and Richard were childhood friends who both had security teams. She would need to meet the men and ladies on Richard's team and Richard would make sure that she would.

Settling down on Daci's couch, Cullea curled up, a cup of tea in her hand. It was late at night and as exhausted as she was, she wasn't ready to sleep. She turned her phone back to face her from where she had left it on the side table. A smile crossed Cullea's face. Caleb had sent a good night text with hearts and flower icons. She had also received a voice mail from the lady who would be her supervisor at the hospital. Cullea was grateful for that, knowing that as dangerous as she felt herself to be, she was welcomed into a new workplace. She was quite looking forward to that.

Daci curled up on the other end of the couch. The day had been exhAidang for them all but she realized that it was more exhAidang for her friend.

"Cullea? You're okay with this?" Daci prayed for Cullea even as she asked the question.

"I am, Daci. I would never have had the nerve to do this. Your friends were great to help."

"It's what we do. Now, we need to go apartment hunting for you at some point. I don't mind you staying here but you'll want your own place at some point."

"I will." Cullea sighed. "I'm just not sure about that. I wish Mom and Dad were here. I need their advice."

"Can we reach out to them somehow?" Daci was ready to do just that.

"Not really. I called the mission, asking if they could get a message to them to let them know that I was all right. They said that they would try. Mom and Dad are in such a remote location that it is hard to get there except to fly in." Cullea grew quiet, her thoughts drifting to the verses on protection and defense that she had memorized in competition with her father. They had that kind of relationship. He would listen to her, support her, but also challenge her to grow.

Daci nodded, knowing that someone from the team or else Aidan had reached out to the mission, asking that very question. They all realized that Cullea was needing her parents. She knew that she needed hers at time, even though they were also away for work.

Not sure what to say next, Cullea simply closed her eyes and began to pray, seeking God's will in how to proceed with the adventure that she seemed to be in. She was worried about Caleb, feeling that he had been hurt because of her. It didn't occur to her that he might be the one who was under attack.

Caleb shifted on his bed, his head aching from the stress of the day. He had not held back in helping his lady. He understood just how stressful it had been for her. Caleb had asked Aidan if he had been able to find a way to bring her parents home. Aidan had nodded and simply stated that he was working on it. He didn't add that he had been in touch with Abe and Abe was willing to fly his team in and bring her parents home.

Chapter 11

A week had passed for Cullea, a week that she needed to try and come to terms with what had happened. She had searched for a car to buy, finding Caleb beside her as she did that. He had simply grinned as she protested, stilling her words when he said that his specialty was vehicles.

Daci had become a close friend as had Payten and Taran. The ladies had simply taken them into their group and spent time praying with her. The consensus had been that they needed to meet for Bible study and prayer once a week. Cullea's face had lit up at that. These were the types of friends that she had prayed for. God had provided that for her.

Joshua had approached her on the Wednesday, a look on his face that she couldn't quite describe. He was grinning at her but she could see the seriousness in his eyes.

"Cullea? You'll be wanting to find your own place. As much as you like living with Daci, you need your own space." He had watched her before looking over at Daci, who was nodding.

"I do enjoy having you here, Cullea. But you need some space of your own. You're used to that. I'm not kicking you out, not at all." Daci wrapped an arm around her friend. "What did you have in mind, Joshua?"

"John Whyte from the church has been watching Cullea. It's in a good way, Cullea. He's on the board of the hospital as well. He knows what happened to you. John has been a good friend to our team. He has an apartment near Caleb that has come up for rent. It has really good security on it. It's on the first floor of a two-story building. He asked me this morning if I thought that you might like to see it."

Cullea stared at him. She had been praying for a place of her own, not expecting one to come up so soon.

"When can I see it?" She had set aside the crutches, her ankle healing enough that she could weight bear with just a brace on it.

"Today, if you like. Caleb is heading this way, he said, as soon as he tidied up." Joshua turned as he heard Caleb's footsteps. "All we have to do is give John a call and he'll meet us there."

"I called him, Joshua. He'll meet us there now, if this is what Cullea wants." Caleb's finger on her lips stopped Cullea's words. "It's what you want to do, Cullea. If you don't want to go tonight or not at all, John understands. You make your decision and we back you, unless it means that you place yourself in danger."

"And just how would I know if I did that?" Cullea's voice was grumpy and she glared at the two men as they laughed. "I mean, I know that I am in danger but I am not receiving all those things that people usually receive."

"No, you're not. You know about those letters that were found at your old apartment. Aidan has the lab working on them. He does want to talk to you about them at some point. That's not tonight. Come on. Let's go see your new abode." Caleb continued to grin at her even as she sighed, reached for her purse, and headed for the door. He was taking over and she wasn't sure that she liked that.

Caleb's hand stopped her forward walk. He bit at his lip, staring at Joshua and then Daci. This had not quite gone as they had prayed.

"Cullea? If you don't want to do this, we don't have to." Caleb waited patiently for Cullea to speak.

Cullea mulled over his words. She sighed once more and turned to apologize, her apology dying on her lips as she studied the tall, handsome man standing in front of her. He was only concerned about her, she knew. Cullea nodded before she walked away from Caleb.

Caleb ran after her, reaching for her hand and tugging her towards his truck. He tucked her inside, finding Daci and Joshua following them.

Walking through the apartment, Cullea felt content and safe. John had gone over the security that he had in place and she was grateful for that. Caleb leaned against a doorway and watched Cullea closely. He could hear Daci and Joshua laughing at something he had said. He turned to study the apartment, walking back through it.

Cullea turned as Caleb wrapped an arm around her. She leaned against him, content to be held. The apartment was just a block from Caleb's home and that was a large factor in her decision to rent it. John had been delighted, he said, to have her as a tenant. He had

---

handed her the keys, waved aside her question about a lease, and told her that it wasn't necessary. If she decided that she needed to move, then they would just do that without any monetary loss to her.

The man who had been following her hit at his steering wheel in frustration. He was under orders to bring both Cullea and Caleb to his employer. There just never seemed to be an opportunity to nab one or the other of them or both of them.

Joshua walked around the building, feeling watched as he did so. He wasn't familiar with that particular block in the neighbourhood and knew that all of the men would be around and become familiar with the neighbours. His eyes took in the vehicles, a frown on his face as he saw the one that seemed out of place. His phone was out as he took a photo of it, moving to catch the license plate number as well.

Caleb approached as he did so, a frown on his face.

"Joshua?"

"That car? It's out of place for the area." Joshua nodded towards the car as it moved away.

"It is, isn't it? Send me the information." Caleb stretched, his hands reaching for the sky before he lowered his arms. "Cullea should be okay in the apartment. John has good security and has agreed that if we need to adjust it, we can."

"He's been a good friend to us over the years. Listen, you haven't said. Have you received any letters or anything like that?"

—

Caleb shook his head. That had puzzled him. He had expected to receive them.

"No, I haven't. That tells me that someone is watching us very closely. Aidan is meeting with us tomorrow night, he said, just to go over what he has. And it's not a lot, he said."

Joshua nodded, having come to that conclusion.

"Any word on her parents?"

Caleb shrugged. He had asked Aidan that when the other man had called him that morning.

"Not yet. He's keeping that very close to himself."

"He is." Joshua turned as he heard the ladies' voices behind him. "All set?"

"We are. John has given me the keys. I guess I have a home in town as well as a job and a vehicle." Cullea paused for a moment. "You know, I haven't had a car for about three months. Mine was an old one and the motor needed too much work. With Mom and Dad away, I just used theirs or walked."

Caleb wrapped an arm around her, his eyes on Joshua who now had a shuttered look on his face.

"No walking right now, sweetheart. If you don't want to drive, call one of us. We'll gladly play chauffeur for you. It's too dangerous. You might disappear and we would never find you."

Cullea turned her face up to watch him before she nodded. She loved walking but knew that she would just herself and anyone around her in danger.

Chapter 12

Two weeks later, Cullea headed for her apartment, locking her car behind her. She was happy, she decided, content in her new work and content with dating Caleb. It was what they had decided to do, date. Cullea knew that it might well be just a cover to draw out whoever it was after them but she was enjoying their dates. Caleb had a sense of humour that was understated at times but it never failed to brighten her day.

She reached for her mail, shut the mailbox door, and headed for her apartment. Closing and locking the door behind her, she dropped her purse in the bedroom and pulled her phone out. Scrolling through the messages, she frowned as she read the one from Caleb. He was delayed, he said, by an unexpected meeting with his team. Could he come by later? Cullea's fingers flew over the keyboard as she agreed.

Changing into favourite casual clothes, Cullea headed for her office. She picked up the mail that she had dropped there. She was disappointed not to have a letter from her parents. Cullea frowned at the envelope that had her name and address on it. There was no return address on it. She dropped it, feeling extreme fear.

Cullea backed up from the desk, her arms wrapping around herself. She turned and ran from the room, finding her phone and calling Aidan. He had not been surprised that she had received a letter. He had been expecting it. He would be there shortly and simply instructed her to keep the doors and windows locked.

Aidan reached for the letter, his eyes on Cullea. He could feel the terror that she was feeling. He frowned for a moment before he looked at the letter. Pulling out the single sheet of folded paper, Aidan raised his eyes once more to Cullea. He had heard the tap at the door and then saw Caleb appearing behind Cullea.

"Cullea? This was in the mail today?"

"It was. I grab my mail or at least check for it every day." Cullea pointed at the paper. "What does it say?"

Aidan unfolded the paper, read it and then folded it, before he stuffed it back into the envelope. He then placed the letter into an evidence bag, dating and signing the bag.

"Aidan?" Caleb spoke at last, his arms wrapping around his lady.

"Cullea, it was a list of everywhere that you have been in the last week, including work, out of meals, shopping. They are following you that closely. They know when you're with someone and when you're not. It's only a matter of time before they do nab you. And if they do it when you're on your own, we may not know for hours." Aidan's voice was stern. He didn't want to frighten Cullea but he knew there was a good possibility that he had.

"I have been? I felt watched but I didn't see anyone. I guess I'm not as alert as I think that I have

---

been." Cullea leaned back against Caleb. "How can I stay safe?"

"By being as aware of your surroundings as you can be. I have a list of people who are willing to protect you when you want to be out on your own. They would not be with you but would be around you. They are officers who want to help you. Don and his team have given much to this community. These officers want to help you."

Cullea felt Caleb nodding. She sighed. This was not what she wanted to hear. She moved away from him, heading for her office. She sank into her chair, her head buried in the arms that she had folded on the desk.

Caleb locked the door after Aidan, knowing that they weren't any further ahead with the investigation. In fact, it was likely going cold and he didn't want that. They just didn't have enough information to move it forward.

He watched with compassion as Cullea sat at her desk. He didn't move towards her. Instead, he headed for the kitchen, making tea for her and coffee for himself and then preparing a simple meal for them. He loaded everything on a tray and headed to find her.

Cullea looked up as she heard his footsteps. She had thought that he had left as well and the soft sounds of his footsteps had startled her. She was on her feet, throwing herself at him and finding him just holding her, a prayer whispering in her ear.

"Okay, sweetheart?" Caleb didn't want to let go of her, knowing that he loved her deeply as early as it was in their friendship.

"No, I'm not. I didn't know that they were following me that closely. I'm afraid now to go out anywhere. What did I do to deserve this?" Cullea sat beside him on the loveseat, reaching for her mug of tea.

"We don't know that you did anything. We don't have enough information to determine that." Caleb bit into his sandwich, chewed and swallowed. "What we need to do is to make a list of your friends, your employer and the staff there, your parents and any other relatives that you have, their employers, etc."

"I see. Then, I have that for you. I couldn't sleep last night and worked on that. Will it help?" Cullea was hoping that it would.

"It should. We have a friend that I'll send it on to. Emma finds people and information that she can't explain how she does. She's already reached out to us and asked for that information"

"She has? Then, we'll do that." Cullea chewed away at her sandwich, not realizing that she had finished it and then reached for a second one. She was hungry that day, not having eaten her lunch.

"I'm off tomorrow, sweetheart. Do you work?" Caleb hoped that she was off.

"No, I'm not. I have to work. I enjoy working with the children. It's so different from working with adults and seniors. They have their lives ahead of

—

them. If I can help make their lives easier, then God is working through me."

"He is. And don't forget that you are bathed in prayer. God is in control, sweetheart. He will protect and defend you against your enemies. It may not be exactly how we would want it. We just have to remember that He has a plan and purpose for our lives." Caleb reached to hug his lady, dropping a kiss on her temple.

Chapter 13

Saturday found Cullea curled up on the glider that she had found for her patio. She loved the seat, spending time in it every day. The movement relaxed her and she needed that. Caleb was on his way, she knew, but for now, she was on her own. Cullea's head went back as she listened to the birds singing away and the noise from the crickets that had somehow appeared. She smiled. She was happy and content even though she was in danger. The only thing that would make her happier was to have her parents here. Cullea was deeply worried about them. She didn't like that they were deep in a country where if they needed help, it would be difficult for that help to reach them.

Hearing a knock at her door, Cullea rose and moved that way, locking the French doors behind her. She peeked out the peephole and then opened the door, walking into Caleb's hug. She was falling in love with this man, she decided, but didn't know how he felt towards her.

Caleb looked down at the lady in his arms. He was afraid for her. Emma had been in touch. She had some information that she needed to get to them. Would they be around later this afternoon? Caleb agreed that they would be. Where did she want to meet them? Emma simply said that they would call once they arrived in Oak City.

Cullea turned late that afternoon. Her hand was tight in Caleb's as he walked her towards her home.

She had felt free that day, the first time in months she decided.

"Caleb? Thank you for today." She grinned up at him as he grinned down at her. "I enjoyed it so much. I don't know that I have had such a good time in years."

"We didn't do anything special, sweetheart. Wandered through some shops. Ate at Ben's diner. Spent time in the library. Stood on the banks of the river. Simple things." Caleb unlocked his front door and turned off his security system.

"I know. It's those simple things that make it a wonderful day. Mom and Dad used to do simple` things with me. A breakfast packed and eaten on the way somewhere. A shared meal out in a restaurant. Reading together. That's what life should be like. Spending time with those who you love and who are important to you." Cullea didn't catch the look on Caleb's face as she said that last sentence. His face lit up as he understood what she had said.

"Thank you, sweetheart. You are right. It is the simple things. Dad used to take me fishing, sometimes waking me up to do that. It's the time spent with our friends and family that counts." He reached to plug in the kettle and turn on the coffee pot. "Emma should be here soon."

"She will? I don't know about this, Caleb. I don't know how I will pay her for what she has done." Cullea chewed away at her lower lip, distressed at the thought.

—

"She doesn't expect payment from friends. And she will consider you a friend. We're all friends with Abe's team as is Richard. And Richard and his team are planning on coming through on Monday. It's a holiday so none of us are working." Caleb made her tea, setting the china cup that he had found just for her on the table and then with a hand on her shoulder making her sit.

"No, we don't. I wish this was all over, Caleb. I worry about you." Cullea didn't look up as she said that, not wanting to see rejection on his face.

Caleb gave an inaudible growl and then was kneeling beside her, an arm around her.

"I am not walking away from you, Cullea. Not ever. You're important to me and I don't want to lose your friendship. If it is in God's will for us, I would like to date you and see where it goes. I don't want to lose you."

Cullea had turned to watch him, seeing the sincerity and desire for her friendship on his face. Her hand reached out to rest against his cheek, feeling the end-of-day stubble under her palm.

"Thank you, Caleb. I don't want to lose you as a friend either." She sighed. "And we just have to do this right now, don't we?"

Caleb began to laugh, tumbling backwards as she shoved at him. She grinned at him as he sat up, his arms resting on his upraised knees.

"And we did. Others have as well. We take what precautions that we can. It may mean that we are injured or disappear. That has happened. Just know that we are prayed for all the time. God is there as well. We are never alone. He has stated that He will never leave us or forsake us. That is a promise that we cling to as a team.”

Cullea nodded, her head turning as she heard a knock at the door. She frowned as Caleb was on his feet, heading that way. She sighed. He was doing it again, taking care of her. She had taken care of herself for so many years that it was difficult to let go.

Emma, Kat and Micah watched from the kitchen doorway as Caleb reached to turn Cullea gently around to face them. They exchanged glances, all of them nodding. Caleb had found his lady, they decided, and they would do all they could to protect her.

“Sweetheart, this is Emma. And Micah and Kat are here as well. Micah is one of Abe’s team and Kat is his wife. She has a family tree program that she runs to help solve crimes. She has some information, she says, for you.”

“Hi.” Cullea felt out of place for a moment, not knowing these people. “Welcome to my home.”

Emma simply reached to hug her, a prayer whispering in her ear.

“Thank you for letting us. I understand that you are having an adventure. We like to tag along on those.” Emma pointed to the table. “We brought a meal with us. Just sandwiches, salads, and fruit.”

“Oh, that is wonderful. Thank you. I hadn’t thought that far ahead.” Cullea turned to the cupboard, finding Caleb ahead of her. He grinned at her as he reached for plates and then their utensils.

Laughter filled the room as the meal progressed. Cullea watched closely, seeing how Emma was watching her in return. She sighed. This was not going how that she thought it would go. What had Emma and Kat to tell her? Cullea rose to help clear the table and then turned, finding Kat beside her.

"It's okay to be afraid and uncertain of people, Cullea. We all had what we call adventures. I almost died from a beating. Micah was hurt as well. Emma and Abe? They were married as they finished university and then separated for ten years. So we can understand to a certain extent what you are facing. None of us know exactly what that is like. We want to help solve this for you. Don and his team are good friends. And I understand that Richard's team is coming through soon."

"They are. And thank you. I appreciate your friendship more than you can understand. It's hard to not know who your enemies are and not be able to protect yourself. I find myself looking at everyone around me, even at work, and wondering if they are the ones who hurt Caleb and are hunting me." Cullea wiped at her face, clearing away the tears. "Now, I understand that you have material to go over with us."

Chapter 14

Emma sat for a moment, her hands resting on the file folders on her knee. Her eyes were on Cullea as she perched on the edge of her desk chair. Caleb had drawn a chair around to sit beside her.

Micah had been watching them as well before his head bowed and he began to pray. Cullea stared at him for a moment before she too bowed her head. She appreciated the prayers more than she could even express.

Emma's head raised as she looked around the room. She liked the comfort of it, clean and neat as it was. She nodded. Cullea was perfect for Caleb.

"Emma? What do you have for me?" Cullea's voice was barely audible.

Nodding, Emma opened the top file folder and handed over the papers.

"This. This is on your parents, Cullea. You have a wonderful set of parents. They are well thought of in the church and community. We found nothing negative about them.

"Your grandparents on both sides were the same. You have a wonderful, Godly heritage that not everyone has." Emma smiled when Cullea nodded and wiped at the tears that had fallen.

"Now, your employer? You worked for him since you graduated?"

"I did. There were not a lot of opportunities for my line of work in that town. I wasn't ready to move to another town. I probably should have. Why?"

"Because he is not on the up and up as we say. There have been rumours about him in the last few years that we are working to confirm or deny. This involves insurance fraud."

"Insurance fraud?" Cullea wrinkled her brow before she shrugged. "I would have no idea. I saw the patients who I was to see. I don't remember seeing the names for any that I didn't see."

"That's what one of your former coworkers has told us. I can't do into any details as it has now become a police investigation. The investigator will be in touch with you. We'll continue to work it as well. Anything we find will be confirmed. You will receive copies as will Aidan."

Kat nodded, her own hands opening a file folder.

"Now, this is your family tree, Cullea. You have some interesting ancestors, did you know that?" Kat grinned as Cullea stared at her. "Didn't know that? I have included that information as well. Caleb? Here's yours. You have some interesting ancestors as well."

The trio walked away shortly afterwards. Caleb locked the door again and went searching for his lady. He wrapped her into his arms, praying for her. Then they just stood, staring at one another. Neither was sure where their relationship was heading but they both knew that they didn't want to walk away from one another.

—

Monday found Cullea turning in Don's work office to face Daci. Daci had tracked her down, simply asking how her work was going.

"It's great, Daci. I wish that I had made that change years ago." Cullea hugged her friend. "Now, what happens today?"

"We meet with Richard and his team. We go over everything that the guys have dug up and that Emma and Kat left. I know that it's going to be stressful. It always is. Now, are you ready to be inundated with people?" Daci had caught Richard standing behind Cullea, a grin on his face. "Richard's team is here. He's right behind you."

"He is? I met him but not his team." Cullea turned to face Richard. "Richard? What are you up to?"

"Helping you and Caleb. I hear that we're meeting in the board room. Have you found that room yet?"

Cullea nodded, hesitating for a moment. A sudden flash of memory hit her and she frowned again before she shook her head. Caleb was waiting for her, a hand held out for her. She gripped his tightly, knowing that the next few hours would change what she knew and felt. She once more prayed to have her parents there, knowing that they couldn't be.

Her head was spinning with information by the time late afternoon came. She didn't know how they had managed to find that much information on herself and her family and then look into those around them. She sighed before she was on her feet and walking

—

outside. Cullea needed some fresh air and some alone time just to try and absorb what she had learned. She knew that one of the ladies from Richard's team, Silver, had been transcribing it all. She just felt too overwhelmed.

Not hearing the vehicles that had approached the building, Cullea jumped and gave a small scream as she heard a voice nearby. She spun, her eyes huge as she stared at Micah.

Micah had a grin on his face even though it didn't quite reach his eyes. She saw men gathering behind him and frowned even as she walked towards him. Caleb was there suddenly reaching for her hand. His grip was warm and tight on hers, signalling his love to her. Cullea wondered at that afterwards.

"Micah? You're here? Did Emma send more information?"

"No, actually, she didn't, Cullea. Abe, Ian, and four of our team headed overseas the day that we were here. They're back. They have a special delivery for you." Micah stepped to one side as the men gathered behind him parted to allow an older couple to move forward.

Cullea's steps stopped as her hands covered her mouth. She blinked rapidly a few times before with a sob, she was running towards them, her hand tugged from Caleb's grip.

"Mom! Dad!" Her sobs shook the men and the ladies watching.

Abe nodded at Don as he moved that way. The men and ladies milled around before they headed into the building. Caleb simply stood and watched his lady with her parents.

Cullea stepped backwards from her parents and directly into Caleb. His arms surrounded her and wrapped her close to him. His eyes were on the couple in front of him, seeing the stress that they were trying to hide.

Cowan and Casee Cassidy studied their daughter and then the man holding her. They frowned at one another. This was not their daughter to let a man hold her like that. Abe had spoken with them in general terms, explaining that Cullea was in danger and that Caleb was one of the men on a security team who was trying to help her out.

"Hi. You must be Cowan and Casee. I'm Caleb. I'm a friend of Cullea's. Welcome home." His hand was out to shake theirs. "How be we head for Don's home?" He nodded that way. "He's okay with that."

They walked that way, Cullea between her parents with their arms around one another. Caleb looked up to see Don and Daci waiting for them. He would need to find Abe later and thank him but when he looked around, he saw that they had already left. It was what Abe did. He would reach out to help and then disappear. His team wanted no thanks for what they felt God wanted them to do.

Chapter 15

Cullea moved quietly around her apartment that night. Her parents had taken the second bedroom just for the night, they said. They wanted to spend time with her and knew that her home was in Oak City. She had not been prepared to see them and had grown very afraid for them. It had been one thing to have them overseas and somewhat safe. It was another thing to have them here in Oak City and at the mercy of whoever it was that was after her.

Caleb paced through the downtown area of Oak City the next afternoon. He was done work for the day and had volunteered to take a package to the mission there for Don. Don had shaken his head, opened his mouth to refuse the offer, and then shut his mouth. Caleb could assess the danger just as well as any of them. He would be alert the whole time.

He didn't hear the running footsteps that approached him from behind. By the time that he realized that someone was running towards him, Caleb was on the sidewalk, his arms tied behind him. Hauled to his feet, he was shoved forward and into an abandoned building. Shoved against the rough brick wall, his head was held there as hands landed on his head and back. Caleb struggled to escape but was unable to do so.

Caleb was held there for many minutes before he was jerked roughly from the area and shoved once more outside and then into a car. He looked around,

—

not recognizing the men and not seeing anyone who would know him and be able to help him.

Sinking back against the seat, Caleb's eyes moved as he tracked where the car was going. The sudden dropping of a blindfold over his eyes startled him and made him jerk before the world went dark. He could no longer see where they were heading. And he felt the car turning in a number of directions, causing him to lose his own sense of direction and to be unable to follow where they were heading.

Pulled roughly from the car, Caleb stumbled as he tried to keep to his feet. He could hear the sounds of nature in his ears and knew that he was near the edge of town or else was outside of it. He prayed for his lady and that she would be kept safe.

Cullea waited for Caleb to appear that afternoon. She paced her apartment moving from window to window to door to door. He just didn't appear. Her parents had headed home, much to her dismay. Her father had hugged her and told her that they needed to but that they would be back by the end of the week. Their mission had asked that of them, that they take a break for a few weeks and spent it with Cullea. Their daughter needed them at this point.

The next morning, Don looked towards the door as the team gathered for their daily meeting. The team that was in for training was due in shortly.

"Where's Caleb?" Don was on his feet, heading for Caleb's office. The room was still dark. There was no evidence that he had arrived.

"He's not in? He was going to be in early this morning, he said as he left." Mark was running for the door and his truck. He wasn't on the list for training that morning. Paul was beside him.

Heading for Caleb's home, the men searched outside of the home. They didn't have a key to his door. There was no sign of him. Mark reached for his phone. He had a bad feeling in his stomach that Caleb had disappeared.

"Aidan? Are you on duty today?" Mark could hear the sound of traffic echoing over the phone.

"I'm on my way in to the office. Why?" Aidan knew that Mark would not be calling him unless something was wrong.

"Caleb is missing. We haven't seen him since he left yesterday afternoon. He didn't show up for training this morning. We're at his home and there's no sign of him or his truck." Mark turned as Paul spoke. "Paul said that he was heading for the downtown area yesterday afternoon to drop off a parcel at the mission."

"He was. Okay. I'll head that way. One of you find Cullea and make sure that she is okay. Stay with her if you can. I know that the hospital is aware of her situation and sometimes someone may need to be with her."

"That's where we're heading." Mark dropped his phone into a cupholder on the console. "Aidan's heading for the downtown area. He wants one of us with Cullea."

"Drop me off there and then head for Don. We'll need to start looking for him. I don't like this, Mark. It's been over twelve hours since we saw him."

Paul ran for the front entrance of the hospital, stopping a security guard as he entered the building. The guard pointed him in the direction that he needed to go. He was familiar with Don's team. He just didn't know that Cullea was part of that team's extended family. In the short time that Cullea had worked there, she had become familiar with the security personnel, knowing that she might need their help at some point.

Paul found a seat in the corner of the waiting room, tucking himself away until he could speak with Cullea. He had stopped and spoken with the clerk who had nodded and told him that Cullea was with a patient and would be for a while.

Walking out with the young girl and her mother, Cullea smiled at the girl's chatter. She was a sweetheart, she decided, and so eager to do whatever it was that Cullea had asked of her. Her eyes raised as she saw Paul and her heart dropped. He would not be here until something had happened. She was suddenly afraid for Caleb. She had been unable to reach him the night before or even that morning. Cullea had stopped trying at last, not wanting to overwhelm Caleb with any messages.

"Paul?" Cullea waited until he walked towards her. "It's Caleb?"

"It is. Where can we talk, Cullea?" Paul followed her back to her office, shutting the door behind him. "When did you last speak with him?"

—

"That would have been yesterday afternoon. He left me a voice mail message just stating that he was heading off on a task for Don and would see me when I finished work. He didn't show up and I haven't been able to reach him." Cullea sank into her chair, her legs not able to support her. "He's missing."

"He is. We'll be looking for him. Mark spoke with Aidan and Aidan was heading for where we know he was last." Paul watched with compassion as Cullea struggled with her tears.

"I see. You're here for now, aren't you?" Cullea knew that without Paul nodding to confirm it. "Okay. I have patients until around three. Then I have paperwork to do. Let me get through the day and then we'll talk. I pray by that time that Caleb is home."

Paul was on his feet. Heading back to the waiting room, he knew it would be a long day for Cullea. He was there until someone showed up to take them to Cullea's home. Whether she stayed there or not would depend on what was found.

Chapter 16

Walking out between Don and Paul that afternoon, Cullea searched the pedestrians that moved around them. She was afraid, she had to admit to herself, more afraid that she had been. Caleb had not been found, that fact she had been advised of. Aidan had been around on her lunch hour and had spoken with her. Cullea had looked up when he had appeared, hope on the face that Caleb was okay before that emotion died away, leaving her face white with fear.

Don walked through her apartment, searching for anything that should not be there. Paul stood on her patio, searching the outside. Nothing was out of place. And Cullea had searched through the few pieces of mail that she had received, not seeing any notes or anything.

Watching Cullea as she made herself a cup of tea, Don shook his head. This was not to have happened, he decided. Caleb had made it to the mission and was heading back to his truck. That much they had been told. As to what had happened to him? No one could tell them. And Caleb's truck was also missing. They just weren't sure if Caleb had been the one moving it. Somehow, none of them thought that.

Cullea turned as Don approached her, fear for Caleb uppermost in her mind. She had reached out to her parents and they were on their way. It would take an hour or so she knew for them to get there.

"Don? Where is he?"

"I don't know, Cullea. If I did, I would walk in and bring him back to you. I just don't know. No one seems to have seen what happened." And to Don's mind, that was unusual. Nothing was missed on the street. That meant that either no one saw what happened or that whoever had seen it was deeply afraid of the men who had likely attacked Caleb. All he could do was pray that Caleb was still alive.

"Is he alive?" Cullea was deeply afraid that Caleb had been killed and his body dumped somewhere he would never be found.

"We have to believe that, Cullea. God isn't done with him yet. I can assure you of that fact." Don reached to hug her. "We'll stay for now until your parents arrive. And when you leave in the morning? One of us will be here and will stay with you during the day. If one of my team can't, Richard or Abe will free up some of them men. Caleb was likely taken to get to you."

"I don't see that, Don. I really don't." Cullea walked away from him, the bedroom door clicking closed behind her.

Don watched her walk away from him, his head shaking as she did so. He needed to talk with her. Only it didn't seem that would be happening.

Mark watched Don before he turned to study the rooms. He wasn't sure if something was off or not. He wasn't familiar enough with her place.

"Don? What do we do? How do we find Caleb?"

—

"I don't know, Mark. I really don't know. I would have thought that we would have received a ransom note or something. I heard that his parents are almost home."

"They are. I spoke with his dad last night. He called just to get my take on Caleb. He's not sure how to read him right now."

"No, Caleb has been different. It's to be expected, going through what he is with Cullea." Don watched as Cullea walked towards them. "Cullea?"

"Where is he, Don? And who did this?" Cullea was having trouble trusting God at the moment. She felt as if she had been abandoned by Him even though she knew that wasn't correct.

"Everyone is looking for him, Cullea. We'll find him." Don excused himself to take a call, surprised to hear from Abe. "Abe? You're calling me?"

"I am. Word has reached our streets that Caleb is missing."

"He is. He went missing yesterday afternoon. We didn't know that until this morning when he didn't show up." Don watched Cullea as she just stood, her arms wrapped around herself. "Cullea is hurting."

"I am sure that she is. Emma has a line on an address. She wants to confirm some more information. We'll be the ones moving in, Don, not you or Richard." Abe hung up abruptly, reaching for the paperwork that Emma was waving at him. "This is where he is?"

"It is. Go on, Abe. Move in and bring him home. Cullea needs him." Emma walked away, her thoughts already on something else.

Don pocketed his phone, a thoughtful look on his face. Mark and Paul studied him and then looked at each other. Something had happened but they knew Don would tell them when he could.

"Cullea? Will you be okay if we leave? We won't if you need us." Don had moved to stand in front of her, his head ducking to watch her face.

"No, it's okay. Mom and Dad should be almost here. Go on. You have things that need to be done. Thank you."

Cullea locked the door behind the three men, her forehead coming down on it. She was unable to stifle her sobs. She wept, fatigue playing into the depths of her despair. She felt the door moving and stepped back. Her parents were there. Casee simply wrapped her daughter into her arms and held her. Cowan moved past them, walking through the apartment and then stopping in the kitchen. He turned on the coffee pot and set the kettle to heat.

Cullea stepped back from her mother once she was able to control her weeping. Casee's hand tucked her daughter's hair behind her ear before she looked up at Cowan.

"Any word yet, Cullea?" Cowan spoke from behind his daughter.

"Not yet, Dad. I just want him home. I need him." Cullea drew in a quivering breath. "I know God

—

is here in this and is in control. It is sometimes hard to see and understand that He is.”

“It is, Cullea. It really is. We know that from experience.” Cowan’s arm was around his daughter’s shoulders. “Here. I’ve made your tea. Sit and we’ll pray this through.”

“Thanks, Dad. I have missed your prayers.” Cullea sipped at her tea before she looked at her father once more. “Dad? What would you do?”

“What would I do? That’s a good question, Cullea. I can tell you what I would do. Your mom could tell you what she would do. What we say may help you but this is a unique situation for you. You are struggling to trust God and that He understands. Just remember that He never leaves you or forsakes you. He hides you under His wings and covers you with His hands. We don’t know where Caleb is or why he was taken. We might never completely understand that. But I do know that God is in control. He has a plan and purpose for you both that we don’t understand or see at this time and place. We may never know that.”

Cullea had her eyes on her father. These were words that he had said before but today? They made more sense.

“Mom?” Cullea turned to her mother.

Casee’s hand was out to cover her daughter’s. She shared a look with her husband before she simply prayed for Cullea.

“I can’t tell you more than what your father has said. It’s hard, Cullea, to trust. God puts us in situations and troubles that cause us to lean on Him and Him alone. As it says, we need to lean on the everlasting arms. He never tires or grows weak or weary of us doing that."

"I get that, Mom and Dad. It's just hard to trust when Caleb is not here. I don't know if he is even alive or dead."

Chapter 17

Two days later, Cullea turned from her living room window. There had been no sign of Caleb despite everyone searching for him. That frustrated and worried her. His team mates had been around, ensuring that she was managing and coping and just praying with her. Daci, Payten, and Taran had spent time with her as well. They were all worried about Caleb.

Don paced his home office that night. He was worried about Caleb. Aidan had been around, not with any news of where Caleb was. Richard had been in touch as had Abe. Both of those teams were searching on their own time. Their ladies had all been in touch with Cullea, just to support her in her worry. They all knew what it was like to be afraid for their fellows.

Turning as he heard a knock at the door, Don opened it to find Kaelen, Aidan, and Toryn there. He simply pointed towards the kitchen. He had just made a fresh pot of coffee and with the looks on the three men's faces, he knew that they would need it.

"Aidan? You have news?" Don sat at his table, his hands wrapped around his coffee mug.

"We do. A friend on the street has been watching for Caleb. They have provided names to us which the team is working through. Abe has been in touch as well. Emma has some addresses for them to search." Aidan rubbed at his cheek. "We'll find him, Don."

"And we don't know what shape that he will be in, will we?" Don sighed, knowing that they were doing everything that they could to find Caleb. "I worry about Cullea. This is not making any sense."

"No, it's not." Toryn nodded before he sipped at his coffee. "We are here as friends, Don, to support you. Your team is out looking. The ladies are with Cullea."

Kaelen looked up at that point, his eyes on Don.

"Don? Have you any sense of why? It's not making any sense."

"No, it's not. I don't know why. None of us seem to have any idea." Don's eyes closed for a moment as he thought through what he knew about Caleb's life. "He's not one to make enemies. None of us are. But someone does hate him to some extent to do this. And I don't get why Cullea is involved. They didn't know one another beforehand. They just ended up on the Bruce Trail at the same time."

"That they were. Someone is watching Caleb very closely." Aidan was on his feet, his phone out to take a call. He turned to watch the three men in the kitchen, hearing their conversation even as he waited for his call to connect.

"Aidan? It's Murphy." Murphy was one of Abe's team and also his business partner.

"Murphy? You're calling? I hope that it's not bad news." Aidan was worried about Caleb.

"We are on site at one of the addresses. We need your patrol vehicles to move in. We have confirmation that Caleb is here. Your judge has a search warrant ready for you." Murphy gave the address where they were located.

Aidan pocketed his phone. He wanted to be there but knew that he could not. It would give too much away if he was. With Abe's team finding the address, he would send in patrol officers who search the home. He just prayed that Caleb was unharmed.

Toryn looked up as Aidan sat back down. Unspoken communication happened between the two men. Don watched them, not sure what was happening but something big had. He prayed that Caleb had been found. Caleb's parents were due back in the morning and Don wanted nothing better than to have Caleb home safe and sound to greet them.

Moving in cautiously, the patrol officers surrounded the building. The Emergency Task Force officers moved towards the doors, some at the front and some at the back. Hammering at the door, the team leader had no response. He frowned at the man standing next to him before his hand was on the door knob. The door opened as he slowly and cautiously turned the knob. He could hear the men entering from the back door.

Searching the three-story house, the leader paused at a locked door. The officer beside him shrugged before they battered at the door, breaking it down. Once inside, they searched the room, worried that Caleb would not be there.

Caleb's head raised as he vaguely heard sounds around him. He was beaten down in spirit and body.

—

The words spewed at him over the last day had done that. Deprived of food and water, his body was shutting down to some degree. That led to his despair.

The officer who had broken down the door was beside Caleb, assessing him. He stood, reaching to help Caleb to his feet and, then with Caleb's arm around his shoulders, led him from the room and carefully down the stairs. A paramedic team was on standby, waiting for Caleb to appear.

Abe watched as Caleb was led from the building and then disappeared into the paramedic rig. He nodded to his team before they walked away to their vehicles. Their work was done. Emma had forwarded her investigative results to Aidan. He sighed. This was getting old, he decided. Too many of their friends had faced danger. *Lord, we need this to end. One of these days, one of our friends will die and leave a devastated family. Protect each one of them. Defend them against their enemies. Thank you.*

Aidan excused himself as his phone chimed. He walked outside, needing the privacy that was offered him.

"Talk to me." His words were clipped. His heart was afraid that Caleb was dead and that meant that he would have to deal with devastated parents and a lady who was falling in love with Caleb right in front of their eyes.

"We have him. He's on his way to the hospital." The officer watched as the paramedic rig pulled away from the crime scene. The officers would be there for a while.

—

"He is? Thanks." Aidan pocketed his phone, his face raised to the sky. *Thank you, Lord. Caleb is alive and back with us. Now to get Cullea there. His parents should be landing soon. I'll send an officer to find them.*

Toryn walked towards him, seeking answers from Aidan.

"Caleb's alive, Toryn, and on his way in." Aidan grinned as Toryn smiled widely. "Abe and his team came through once more."

"That they did. Now, we need to find Cullea and get them back together." Toryn paused. "We need to find someone for Caleb to speak with."

"And we will. We have a vast resource list for that." Aidan walked away, leaving Toryn to head back into the house. He was on a mission to find a lady and reunite her with her defender.

Chapter 18

Cullea turned from her window. She had been watching for Caleb to appear. She just didn't think that he would. A tap at her front door had her heading that way, pulling open the door to see Aidan standing there. Fear rose in Cullea's heart.

"He's dead, isn't he? Caleb is dead." Cullea was working herself into a frenzy.

Aidan wrapped her into a hug, waiting for her to calm down somewhat.

"He's alive, Cullea. He's at the hospital. I'm here to take you to him." Aidan waited patiently as she composed herself. "Come on. Find your phone and your purse. We'll head off to find your guy."

Cullea frowned at him for a moment, her mouth open to deny that Caleb was her guy. She snapped it closed and turned to reach for her purse. Her keys were taken from her hands as Aidan locked up after her.

"His parents? Are they there?" Cullea wanted to meet them but was also afraid to. She was sure that she was the reason for the danger and harm that had threatened him

"They landed a while ago. Kaelen and Don headed to find them. They'll get his parents to the hospital. For now, you're with me. I'll get you in to see him."

Calum and Caiti Campion paced the waiting room at the hospital. Kaelen and Don had met them at

---

the hospital, concern for them uppermost in their minds. The older couple had hugged their son's friends and then stood back, their eyes searching their faces.

"Don? You have word?" Calum broke the silence at last, his arm around his wife.

"We do. Caleb is at the hospital. I haven't heard how he is or what is wrong. We'll head there with you." Don reached for some of their luggage, Kaelen taking the remainder. The two men shook their heads as the couple protested.

"Wait, Don. What about the lady who you said was involved?" Caiti refused to get into Don's truck without him responding.

"She's okay and safe. Aidan is with her at the hospital. She'll want to see Caleb as well. They're a couple whether they agree that they are or not." Don grinned at the couple.

"A couple, you say?" Calum thought it through and then nodded. That would be his son, he knew.

Don led them into the waiting room of the Emergency department, searching for Cullea. Finding her, he pointed towards her.

"That's Cullea. I'm not sure if you have ever met her."

Caiti studied her and then shook her head. She didn't think that Cullea was known to them. She walked towards the young lady who spun as she heard footsteps, her eyes huge.

—

"Cullea? May I call you that?" Caiti waited for Cullea to nod before she wrapped her into a hug.

"I'm sorry. I don't think that I know you." Cullea's frown darkened her face.

"No, I don't know that we do. I'm Caleb's mother. We were just back today. This is Caleb's dad, Calum."

Calum hugged Cullea before his arm was around his wife. He found seats for the two ladies before he turned to Aidan, who stood nearby.

"Aidan? Talk to me. Tell me what happened." Caleb was an international representative for a local manufacturing company. Caiti and he had been overseas for the last couple of months, sourcing new contacts for that company.

"Our ETF and some patrol officers went in and found him today. He's here, being assessed. I need to talk to him before I have any idea of what he went through." Aidan's hand rested on Calum's shoulder. "Let me pray with you before I head back there again. He was being assessed. I'll make sure that they know you're both here. They know that Cullea is here. She made sure that they did." A smile cracked across Aidan's face as he remembered how Cullea had not backed down from the clerk.

"She did, did she? How close are they? We haven't had much contact with Caleb in the last few weeks. We've been on the move too much, I think."

"You have been. You need to stay home for a while, Calum, and let someone younger travel."

"I know. We're working towards that, Aidan." He pointed towards the door. "Head on back. Come and find us when you're able to."

Calum paced to the outdoors. Spending hours on a flight had not been in their plans for the day. When word reached them through his office that Caleb had disappeared, there had been no question that they would head for home. Caiti would have returned on her own if he hadn't just packed up and came with her.

Toryn approached him, a hand out to shake Calum's. He simply stood with the older man. Calum was a great friend to his son's friends. He was always ready to spend time with them, whether it was just to listen to them, advise them, or pray with them.

"Toryn? You're doing okay? Work isn't overwhelming you?" Calum had a soft spot in his heart for Toryn, worrying about the police chief who had taken over at a younger age than most.

Toryn nodded, not sure how to respond to that.

"Okay, I guess. No, it's okay. It's just this stuff with Don's team. I worry about them."

"We all do." Calum turned to stare at the hospital building. "It's wearing on their families and their friends. And you know only too well what they are and may face. Better than even their families."

"I do. And I fear for them all. Right now? It's Caleb and Cullea that are in danger. Cullea is struggling. Caleb just wants to keep her safe. They're a couple whether they have acknowledged it to themselves or not."

"That is what we wondered, Caiti and I. I am sure that they are. Caleb would not walk away from her if she's in danger. And in doing so, he would come to care for her very deeply."

Calum walked towards Caiti who had come looking for him, his hand reaching for hers. Toryn followed them, finding Aidan waiting for him.

Chapter 19

Standing at their son's bedside, Caiti had trouble controlling her emotions. Tears wet her cheeks even as Calum wrapped an arm around her. His other arm was wrapped around Cullea, holding her in place beside him. She was uncomfortable with that. Cullea was determined that she should not be there. Caleb's parents had thought otherwise and just swept her into the room with them when the nurse came to find them.

Caleb's eyes flickered open and closed. He felt warm and comfortable and cared for. That was something that he just didn't understand. Convinced that he was still a captive, he didn't want to open his eyes and see his captor standing over him once more. The words that had been hammered at him every few hours still resounded in his mind. The bright lights that had stayed on day and night still shone in his eyes. Caleb could hear the heavy footsteps that had paced around him hour on hour.

"Son?" Caiti's hand rested on her son's head. "It's time to wake up, son. You're safe."

Caleb relaxed as he heard his mother's voice. She couldn't be captive. If she was here, then he was safe, just as she had said.

"Mom? You're home?" Caleb had to clear his throat to be able to speak. His throat was dry. He felt a hand holding up his head and then a straw touching his lips. He sipped, not happy when the glass was removed.

"We are home, son." Calum spoke up at that point. "And we have Cullea here too."

"She is? I thought that she had run away. That's what they told me." Caleb finally opened his eyes, searching the faces surrounding him, his eyes stopping on Cullea. He saw the fear that she was trying to hide and the discomfort.

"Mom? Dad? You weren't to be back yet." Caleb nodded as his mother raised the head of his bed.

"No, we weren't. But you needed us. That takes priority." Calum turned as he heard footsteps. "Aidan is here. We'll leave and let him speak with you."

Caleb nodded, his eyes on Cullea. He reached out his hand and took hers, preventing her from leaving.

"Cullea needs to stay, Aidan. I know that you don't want that, but I need her here." Caleb was adamant about that. He was ready to not tell what had happened to him if Aidan insisted that she not be present.

"She shouldn't be. You know that Caleb. I do need her to leave. She can wait right outside the door where you can see her. But you need to let me have your statement without her in the room." Aidan pointed to the wall outside the room. "Cullea, you stand right there. Caleb can see you but you can't hear what he is saying. We need to do that."

Cullea sighed. It was what she figured he would want. She wanted to stay with him but she couldn't. She both knew and understood that. Moving to rest

———

with her back against the wall, Cullea kept her eyes on Caleb and found that he was watching her as much as he could.

Aidan shook his head. These two were connected, he decided, and needed to be with one another. Only he didn't seem to know when that would happen.

"Okay, Caleb. Tell me what happened." Aidan pulled out his pad and pen and set up his laptop to record Caleb.

"I don't know who it was. I was tackled in the downtown area, taken into one of the buildings, held there, and then shoved into a truck. From there, I was taken to a house just outside of town. I think it's still in your jurisdiction." Caleb was sore and fatigued and not sure if he could even stay awake to finish his statement. "They kept bright lights on all the time. Every hour or so, they would come in and hammer at me that I was no good and that I wasn't worth it. That nobody wanted to know me or be with me. They would stomp around me after they said this. They were trying to wear me down and defeat me."

"That they were. And they succeeded to some extent, even in just a few days." Aidan looked down at his notes. "Do you know who they were?"

Caleb shrugged, puzzled at the question.

"I've seen a couple of them around town in the last couple of months. I don't know who they are. And the others I couldn't say that I had seen at any time." His eyes turned to watch Cullea, finding her standing with her head bowed. She was praying, he knew without being told.

"That's okay. I'll have you come into the station tomorrow and work with a police artist." Aidan tucked everything away and left, stopping by Cullea for a moment. She stared at him, her eyes shuttered. He sighed to himself, something he knew that he was doing a lot lately.

Cullea walked away from him and back into the exam room, right into Caleb's arms. He held her tightly, not wanting to let her go. His head rested against her.

"I missed you, sweetheart. I was so worried about you." Caleb's voice held all the love for her that had developed.

Cullea froze in place, her arms around Caleb's neck. She leaned back to look at him, a frown on her face that smoothed out as she saw the love on his face.

"Caleb? What are you saying? It's not in your words." Cullea wasn't sure what she was reading.

"Cullea? I was so worried that you would disappear. I couldn't handle that. I love you." Caleb knew that he was putting himself out there.

"You do? Caleb, when would you have told me?" Cullea could hear footsteps passing by the room, echoing in the hallway.

"I didn't want to do it this way, sweetheart. I love you more than anyone. When I was gone, I missed you and worried about you so much." Without thinking, he kissed her, finding her responding. "Cullea?"

"I love you too, Caleb. I didn't know that you loved me." Cullea snuggled closer to him, finding him swinging his legs over the side of the stretcher to gather her closer to himself.

"You do? That's wonderful, sweetheart. We'll talk. Right now, I want my discharge papers and to leave. My parents are here. Yours are likely as well. And I want to spend time with my lady love and my families." Caleb grinned down at her for a moment, his eyes rising as he heard footsteps. "Don?"

"Ready to leave, Caleb? Cullea?" Don just grinned at them. "We have vehicles waiting for you. Aidan has arranged an escort for us. Your parents are heading home, Caleb, but will be at your place shortly."

Chapter 20

Caleb and Caiti stood for a moment watching their son as he walked towards them, Cullea's hand tight in his. They shared a look with Caiti nodding. The couple had reached an agreement of some sort, she acknowledged to herself. From what she could see, they suited one another. Cullea's parents stood beside them. The couples realized that they did know one another from church, just not that well. Casee knew that would change. She could read her daughter. Cowan stared at them as well before he turned to Don.

"They've made a decision, Don."

Don smiled even as he agreed. They had made a commitment to one another. He just didn't think that they would tell them that day. It would come. It was up to Don and his team to keep them safe. With Caleb as one of their team, it would be more difficult but they had done that with both Paul and Thomas.

Late that night, Caleb paced his house. He was unable to settle down. The last few days had done that to him. He felt threatened all the time. Caleb wasn't sure how he would even continue working on the team. Reaching for his phone, he read his text messages. His team had all been in touch as had Richard and his team and Abe and his team.

Caleb tossed his phone on the couch, curling up to try and sleep. His thoughts went to Cullea and he smiled for the first time since he had arrived home. He had sent his parents home and also his team members.

___

He wanted to be on his own. Caleb was afraid to be around anyone.

A knock at the door disturbed him. He didn't rise, praying that whoever it was would disappear. That didn't work as another knock came at the door. He rose, heading that way, feeling grumpy and out of sorts.

Kaelen and Joshua stood there, bags of food in their hands. They both knew that Caleb had probably not eaten.

"What are you two doing here? I want to be on my own." Caleb's grumpiness came out in his words.

"We know you do, but you're not going to be. Now, let's eat. Then we spend a lot of time in prayer for you and Cullea. This is not over, Caleb, not by a long shot." Joshua simply moved past his friend and headed for the kitchen. "You won't have eaten, Caleb. I know you only too well."

Caleb nodded, finding the food that they had provided for him. He ate, not really tasting what it was, but knowing that he had to. He had not eaten in a few days.

Kaelen gathered up the trash and got rid of it in the garbage pail. He poured them all refreshed mugs of coffee. He sat once more, glancing between the two friends.

"Let's pray, Caleb." Joshua bent his head, knowing that they would spend the next while petitioning God. It was what was needed for both

Caleb and Cullea. He could only pray that Cullea had someone to do that with her.

Cullea curled up on the couch at her parents'. They had insisted that she needed to come home with them, if only for the night. She hadn't wanted to but she had. Cullea knew that they were deeply concerned about her and she could not say no.

Casee sat on the other end of the couch, wanting to talk with her daughter but not sure how to go about it. Cowan approached, setting down a tray with refreshments for them. He then found his favourite chair.

"Cullea? I'm going to ask you a question. You don't have to answer unless you wish to." Cowan watched his daughter closely. "What are your feelings for Caleb?"

"My feelings?" Cullea struggled with answering that. She wanted to tell her parents the truth, that the couple loved one another, but it was all so new and fresh that she wanted to keep it to herself for a little while longer. *God, what do I tell them? You have brought Caleb into my life. I thank you for that. I just don't know where this will go.* "My feelings? I love him, Dad. And yes, he loves me. I didn't want to tell you, not just yet."

Casee gave a soft smile. She remembered all too well the feelings of first love and the first moments when it was first acknowledged between a couple.

"That's wonderful, dear. We won't pry as it's too new for you. We just needed to know how to pray for you two. We know better now." Casee reached for her daughter's hand to squeeze it.

"Thanks, Mom. We haven't really talked about it. I know that we will." Cullea sighed, knowing that she had to be totally honest with her parents. "I'm just not sure where this will go. We are in danger but we don't know why or who. And that affects how we live."

"Does it, Cullea?" Cowan broke into the conversation, his father heart hurting for his beloved daughter. "If Cullea were to ask you to marry him tomorrow, what would you say? If you knew that you only have a few weeks together, would you refuse to marry him and live separately or would you take the time that God gives you?"

Cullea knew what her father was saying. It was not something that she had not heard before. She was just too afraid to even consider anything at that moment. Caleb disappearing as he had? That had shaken her beyond what she had expected.

"I'm just afraid, Dad, that someone will hurt Caleb. I don't know who this is that is behind this. We haven't been able to make that determination."

"Does he know where he was held?" Casee watched Cullea struggle before she spoke.

"He does. He told me who. I know that Aidan is aware of it. I just don't know where to go from here." Cullea told them the name, drawing exclamations of surprise from her parents. "It's not who I expected it to be. And we don't know if he's involved or if his place was just used."

———

Cowan had been surprised at the name before he nodded. He knew the man and knew that he walked very close to the line or over the line in criminal activities. He hid it well. Cowan had had dealings with him years ago and that had not gone well for the man. He suspected that the man was after Cullea to retaliate. He would need to talk with Calum to find out what he knew.

"We'll pray for you both, love. And we will work on this. I have a friend who I can call in. He'll be glad to help." Cowan knew that he would reach out to a friend who lived in Mistletoe. He also knew that Don had reached out to his friends. Somehow, between all of them, they would solve this and hopefully, God willing, before either of the couple was hurt or killed.

Chapter 21

The next morning, Caleb walked slowly towards their office building. He really didn't want to be there. Even with Joshua and Kaelen staying with him the night before and spending many hours in prayer, he was not ready to go back to work. And that hurt big time. Caleb loved his work, dealing with the ins and outs of the vehicles needed for security. It was more complex than most people thought and he liked that challenge

Don motioned for him to head for Don's office. Don needed to assess Caleb and where he stood in relation to his work. His disappearance for those few days had worried him deeply.

"Caleb? Just how are you?" Don would probe and probe deeply. His team knew that only too well.

Caleb shrugged, not sure how to express what he thought and how he felt.

"I'm not sure, Don. I'm hurting in many ways. I am going to speak with someone today." Caleb rubbed at his face. "Have you any thoughts on why?"

"No, not really. We're working on it but there is just one detail or name that we don't have. Do you know any of the men who held you?"

"No, I don't. I've seen a couple of them around town. We could go to the street and ask. I'm sure that they would be willing to help."

"We're already receiving names from them. Here's the list." Don handed over a paper, his eyes rising to the doorway where the other four team members stood. He beckoned them in.

"I don't recognize any of the names. They were very careful not to call one another by name. If I had photos to go with the names, then I could tell you who they were." He looked around as Mark reached for the paper. He was surprised that they were all there but he shouldn't have been.

Mark studied the names before he reached for the second computer in Don's office. He was away on a search, pulling up names and addresses as well as photos of the men. He printed them off and handed them around to the others.

All eyes studied the men and then each other. They knew the men and that wasn't good. The men had tried to come in as a security team trainees and had been refused. There had been red flags.

"So, this is connected to our work? There must be more to that." Caleb dropped the papers on the desk and bowed his head. He prayed for his lady, wanting to find her and just hold her.

The men shared looks before Mark sent the information on to Aidan and then to Emma. Those two would work on it and determine what needed to be done after that. The problem in the meantime was keeping Caleb safe and then keeping Cullea safe. They just weren't sure how to do that.

Cullea wondered her yard that afternoon. She had moved from the apartment to a small house that

John had for rent. He had been glad to let her have it. She needed to find work, she decided, something that would keep her occupied. Her last position? She had been ready to move on, she knew. Cullea just wasn't sure what to do now. She turned as she heard a noise, a frown on her face. She couldn't see anyone. Strong fear made her race for her home, slamming the door and locking it after herself. She set the alarm system and checked all the doors and windows.

She could hear the pounding at her doors and then the hands hitting on her windows. She shrank back and desperately looked for somewhere to hide. Cullea dove into her closet, pulling clothing in front of her, praying that it would be enough.

The screaming of her security system made her jump and then clamp a hand over her mouth to stifle her scream of fear. Her other hand clutched at the clothing. She prayed hard, begging God for protection and a defense. The sound of running footsteps through her home and the opening and slamming of doors came closer to her. The door to the closet pulled open and some of the hangars were moved. She could see dirty sneakers in her line of sight as she stared at the floor, her heart pounding with fear.

There were loud and angry voices but she was too afraid to listen to the words. The sneakers disappeared as running footsteps once more sounded in the house. The sounds of emergency vehicle sirens also came to her.

Sinking to the floor of the closet, Cullea buried her head against her knees, shrinking back into a corner. Her arms were wrapped around her head. She didn't hear the officers walking through her home, searching for anyone that should not be there but more importantly searching for her.

Aidan stood at the front door. He studied the broken-in door. He turned as Don and Caleb approached him, seeing the worry and fear on Caleb's face.

"Aidan? What happened?" Don stopped, a hand reaching out to stop Caleb's forward walk.

"Someone broke into Cullea's. We haven't found her yet so we don't know if they succeeded in finding her." Aidan was watching Caleb. "Caleb? I'll let you walk through to see if you can find her hidden somewhere. Other than her parents, you are likely the one who knows her home best. I spoke with her parents. They're back in her hometown."

Caleb nodded, hesitating to pray for his lady. He was deeply afraid that she had disappeared.

"Aidan, you need to be with me. That way, no one can say that I disturbed or changed any evidence."

Aidan nodded himself, knowing that Caleb was correct.

"Let's find your lady, Caleb."

The two men walked into the house, searching room by room, moving objects in closets. Aidan looked for access to the attic, not seeing a trap door.

"The attic?" Aidan kept his voice low.

"Through the garage. There's a trap door there." Caleb turned for a moment, intending on heading that way. "We just have the master bedroom to search." He headed that way, his prayer that she was there.

Caleb stood for a moment, staring around. Aidan had bent to look under the bed and raised back up, shaking his head. He pointed silently to the closet. The door was open, something that Caleb knew Cullea would never do.

He reached for the clothing and stopped. Instead, he bent over, searching. A small cry came from him before he was on his knees, reaching for Cullea.

Cullea fought him, certain that the men had found her. It took a few moments for her to realize that it was Caleb that was holding her, trapping her arms to her sides to prevent being hit.

"Cullea? You're okay?" Caleb's voice was barely a whisper in her ears as he loosened his arms and just swept her into his arms. On his feet, he headed for the door, Aidan following him.

Aidan was never sure afterwards how Cullea had avoided the men. He knew from the shape the house was in that they had searched for her, not caring that they damaged or destroyed anything in their way. Cullea had shaken her head at him and told him that God had put an angel in front of her. She had seen that form defending her. The men shared a look and then nodded. God would and could do just that.

Chapter 22

Cullea just refused to leave Caleb, not that he was letting go of her. He set her in Don's truck and stood at the open door, an arm around her. Aidan studied him and then turned back to the house. They would be there for a while. That meant Cullea would need to find another place for the night. This was not how their Friday night was to go.

Don approached Caleb, his eyes on Cullea for a moment. He had asked Aidan to retrieve her purse and phone. Daci had been in touch, asking that Cullea come her way. Don wasn't sure where she would end up but she would not be alone. He could tell that Caleb was determined not to leave her.

Richard had appeared, not saying anything but standing side by side with Caleb. Raleigh, his wife, had slipped into the truck beside Cullea, not saying anything but keeping her company.

"Where do you want to go, Cullea?" Don spoke at last.

Cullea shrugged, taking her purse and phone. She wasn't sure where to go or where she would be safe. She felt Caleb's arm tighten around her.

"I don't know, Don. Where can I go?"

"Daci would like you to come to her. If not, perhaps Caleb's parents? I know that their security is very good." Don could see Caleb nodding.

"My parents, I think, Don. That way, we can stay together. They go after one or the other of us if we're on our own." Caleb sighed, knowing that during the week, it wasn't possible for them to actually be together.

"Are you sure?" Don knew full well that Caleb was. He rubbed at his face. This event would mean a meeting with his team. Richard was nodding at him. That meant that Richard's team was weighing in. He just wanted this over and to not have it go through all of his team. They were half-way through the team by now.

Cullea turned to Caleb, finding him watching her in turn. He nodded, reaching to hug her. She clung to him, feeling safe in his arms but knowing that in a few hours they would separate and go their own ways. It was how it worked.

"Don? Can we head that way or are you still needed here?" Caleb's question was low-pitched. He could feel the eyes watching them.

"I need to stay. Richard?" Don turned to his friend, not needing to even ask a question.

"We'll take them, Don. Call me later. We'll see what we can do to help. Abe's weighing in as well." Richard tucked the couple into his truck, searching the area around them. This was a dangerous time for them, transferring them from vehicle to vehicle. He could see Caleb searching as well, senses on high alert.

Calum stood back from the back door, his eyes on his son and Cullea before he reached to shake Richard's hand and then hug Raleigh.

———

"What brings you four here?" He pointed towards the living room. "We're in there, son."

"Thanks, Dad. We're here because someone tried to kidnap Cullea from her home tonight. Can we stay overnight?"

"That goes without saying that you can." Caiti hugged her son and then reached for Cullea, finding the younger lady just clinging to her. "Cullea? Do you want to call your parents?"

Cullea sniffed before she nodded. She needed her mother and she was miles away right now.

"Thank you, Caiti. Maybe in a bit." Cullea was still shaking from fear.

Caleb wrapped her into an arm and led her to a couch, shoving her down and sitting beside her. Raleigh sat on her other side, her eyes shifting between Cullea and Richard.

Richard turned in the kitchen as Calum approached him.

"Richard? What happened? I heard what Caleb said. But I don't understand." Calum was puzzled. All had seemed well with both Cullea and Caleb earlier that day.

"Someone made it into Cullea's house looking for her. She was able to hide, I gather, until Caleb found her. The front door needs to be replaced for one thing. For now, Don and I agree with Aidan. Cullea needs to be with Caleb." Richard had moved to the doorway and then into the hallway where he could stand and watch the couple. "They're a couple, Calum. They need to be together."

"We know that they do. And Cullea needs her mom." Calum worked away as he prepared a simple meal for them all of sandwiches and fruit. Richard moved back into the room to help him.

"We'll get her here. I understand that Mark and Joshua were heading that way to bring them back here." Caiti paused for a moment. "Who is after them and which one is it?"

"That's what we don't know yet, Caiti." Toryn spoke from beside her, causing her to jump. He grinned at her before she hugged him. Toryn was a favourite with them all, simply being there for his friends. His prayers had helped to raise many spirits through the years. Caleb and Toryn had been friends since they were toddlers.

"I wish that I knew. I would go after them and make them stop." Caiti had gone full mother-bear mode, angry that someone was after her son and his lady.

"That's what we don't want you to do, Caiti." Toryn reached for the tray in her hands. "You may not survive if you do."

"We need to find whoever it is. They might not survive." Caiti walked away, leaving the men staring after her before they all shared a look. They know it was only too true that the couple might not.

Cullea looked up as Caleb's arm tightened around her. She knew that they had reached a

———

crossroads in their relationship. She was determined to walk away, to quit her job at the hospital, and move on to another town. Caleb was reading her face and shook his head at her. His arm tightened around her.

"Don't do it, sweetheart. Don't leave me. I can't do it if you do."

Cullea nodded, not sure that she would stay. Her flight instincts were kicked in and that was all she wanted to do. Only Caleb was too important to her. She could not run from him, no matter how much she felt that she should.

Chapter 23

On the following Monday, Cullea dropped her purse into her desk drawer at work and then locked the drawer. She was exhausted, not having slept well that weekend. She had been unable to do so, worried that someone would break into her home again.

Walking through the hospital corridors, Cullea searched each face, not sure if it was a man or woman after her and after Caleb as well. There was just not enough information to figure out who. She knew that Aidan was frustrated as well. What would it take, Cullea wondered, to bring them out into the open?

Pausing at the doorway of her office, Cullea turned for a moment. She had heard footsteps following for the last five minutes but when she turned, there was no one behind her. Cullea was puzzled by that. Her workday over, she simply grabbed her belongings and walked out to where one of Don's team was to be waiting for her. She frowned. No one was there to meet her. She stepped back into the entrance, her eyes searching for someone she knew who was there for her.

Hearing someone stop beside her, Cullea refused to look. She was afraid of that, afraid that someone was here to kidnap her.

"Cullea?" Stephen and Naomi from Richard's team were there. "You're done for the day?"

Cullea drew in a breath of relief. Help was here and not just one person but two.

"I am. I didn't see anyone waiting for me."

"We know. We're parked in the back of the lot. Out this way." Stephen's hand on her arm turned her from the entrance and towards the rear of the hospital. "We've cleared it with security to go this way. The rest of our team is waiting for you."

"Thank you. I hate putting you at risk."

"It's what we do, Cullea. And we are glad to do it for Caleb. Don's team has always been there for us what with Richard and Don being friends from childhood." Naomi grinned at her even as she slid open the van door and waited for Cullea to climb in.

Cullea listened to the light chatter around her, thankful that God had provided for her once more. She frowned as she saw the direction the van was turning.

"This isn't towards my home."

"No, it's not. We're heading for somewhere else tonight, Cullea. We need to make some plans for you and Caleb." Richard turned, a compassionate look on his face. "Don and his team are meeting us there. And yes, Caleb will be there. And your parents are on their way back here. We want to keep all of you in one town. It makes it easier to keep you safe."

Cullea nodded herself, sure that Richard was correct. She did want to see her parents. She needed their counsel.

"Thank you, Richard. I just don't have to like this." Cullea knew that she sounded ungrateful and disgruntled, yet refused to apologize for it.

Caleb was pacing the driveway of the house that Joshua had found for them. He didn't like that it had come to this even though he knew that he would not stay there long. Staying hidden and safe did not solve their adventure. They needed to be out there where they could be found no matter how dangerous it was for them.

Cullea was out of the van and into Caleb's arms, welcoming the strength with which he held her. Her prayer last night had been that he would ask her to be with him for the rest of their lives. She didn't think that it would ever happen.

Caleb turned her and rushed her into the house, closing the door behind him.   Cullea had the impression of many people there, more than what she had expected. She felt hands on her and turned to find her mother there, waiting to wrap her into a mother hug. Cullea felt her father's arms around his two ladies.

Caleb walked away, hunting for Richard who was waiting for him outside in the backyard. Richard was not comfortable with the house, the trees too close to it for his liking. But Don knew his town and knew that Joshua would have been confident in that home for at least the night. Richard also knew that Caleb would not stay there for long nor would Cullea.

"Richard?   Everything went okay?"   Caleb stopped beside him, seeing Don on Richard's other side.

"It did. Cullea was smart enough to come back inside when she didn't see her ride. Not many would have done that. They would have gone searching for that.”

“She’s terrified, Richard. She just doesn’t want anyone to know that. Cullea hides a lot underneath. I am only just now getting her to open up to me. It’s been a struggle. She thinks that someone may have been following her for months. She just didn’t think about it as being that.” Caleb was frustrated and he had every right to be.

“That may well be true, Caleb. Now, what do we do with you? Don?” Richard turned to his lifelong friend to answer that.

“We’ll stay here tonight and make some plans. Thanks for stepping in, Richard. Your team needs to get on the road and head for home. You have a full day tomorrow.”

“That we do, but it’s what we do for one another. Abe’s ready to move in this week if you need him. Emma’s been grumbling about not finding much. That’s unusual for her.”

“It is. Somewhere, there’s a key to this all. We just need to find the key that will unlock the door.” Don walked away, leaving Richard hesitating before he too walked away.

Caleb waited patiently, knowing that one of his team mates would be around soon. Instead, it was Aidan. The detective simply stood by his friend, waiting with him. Neither man was sure what it was that they were waiting for but it was something. Caleb’s heart was heavy with worry and the need to defend his lady. At least, he still prayed that she was his lady. They had not had an opportunity to speak with one another again about that. He prayed for her and for what they were facing. Caleb just wanted it over.

"Aidan? Any word on those men?" Caleb's voice broke through the silence between them.

"No, not much. It's frustrating, Caleb. They have gone into hiding. There are still sightings of them. We know that someone is following both of you. We just can't seem to get there in time to catch them." Aidan was frustrated by that.

"Then, you have a leak or else they have hired someone to watch the police department and monitor the calls."

Aidan nodded. Caleb had gone to the heart of the matter, much as he had expected him to.

"That's what we think, Caleb. That makes it much for dangerous for you two. I have no idea how to keep you two safe. You're with your team during the week. Cullea is at the hospital and security is watching out for her. She has become a valued employee in just a short time. They love her there."

"I know. It's after hours and weekends that we need to watch out for." Caleb turned as he heard a soft sound, simply sweeping Cullea close to him.

Chapter 24

The next day, Cullea walked away from the hospital. She had resigned from her work, not liking that she was putting everyone at risk. Her supervisor had tried to convince her to take a leave of absence. Cullea had simply shaken her head, said no, and left. She had sent Caleb a text that no one was to meet her after work that day. She would be home instead.

Walking rapidly down the street, Cullea was lost in thought. She didn't see the youth following her, his eyes searching for anyone coming to her aid. Not one person was. He grinned to himself. This was what he had been waiting for. His orders were to find her and bring her to his boss.

Cullea could hear the footsteps behind her. She refused to look back. If whoever it was wanted to grab her, she was all for it. She had argued it out with God the night before, finally just telling Him that she knew that He was in control. She may come to harm or even die but He would use that for His glory. He was her Defender even more than Caleb wanted to be.

Moving quickly, Cullea darted into Ben's diner, heading for the kitchen. Caleb had introduced her to Ben one day. Ben had asked her to come and find him if she was in the area and felt unsafe. He would hide her and then get her to safety. Ben looked up and then pointed towards his office. He frowned for a moment as he saw the youth enter and look around, obviously searching for Cullea.

Cullea sank gratefully into a chair. She was afraid, she had to admit to herself, afraid that she would disappear and devastate her family when she never returned. She still had no idea who was after her. Reaching for her phone, Cullea pulled up the messages. It had been vibrating in her purse for the last fifteen minutes and she had just ignored it. A frown covered her face. A lady named Emma had reached out to her. Would Cullea please call her back?

Cullea hesitated for a moment. The name "Emma" sounded familiar but she could not place it.

"Hello?" The rich yet soft voice floated across the airwaves to Cullea.

"Is this Emma?" Cullea's voice was hesitant.

"Yes, it is. And this is Cullea?" Emma was confident that it was. "Cullea, where are you right now?"

"I'm in Ben's diner. I was followed and came in here since Ben had offered to help." Cullea nodded as Ben sat down a mug of tea beside her and walked away, praying for Caleb's lady as he did so.

"Good. You're not on your own. I received word that someone would make an attempt today to grab you. Thank God that you are safe."

"I don't understand how you would know that." Cullea was genuinely puzzled at Emma's words.

"It's what I do, Cullea. I can't explain how it works. I'm not sure that I even understand it myself. But there is someone close to you that is following you. What about your work? Is someone watching out for you there?" Emma heard the hesitation over the line before her mouth opened to ask the question again. She frowned at Abe as he sat in front of her desk, their young son, Isaac, on his knee.

"That's not a problem, Emma. I walked away from it today. I just didn't want to put anyone at risk. So now I have to fill my day and not put myself out there as much as I would like to. I want this over." Cullea blinked rapidly, tears almost getting the best of her.

"You did? You were that sure?" Emma waited patiently for Cullea to answer. She could hear the sounds of what seemed to be Cullea struggling to control her emotions. Emma then began to pray audibly for Cullea.

"Thank you, Emma. I needed that. Now, you had called me. What was it that you wanted?" Cullea set aside her emotions. Emma was a busy lady and she needed to hear what she had to say.

"I did, Cullea. Not for anything in particular other than to warn you to be very careful. Someone is tracking both you and Caleb. We don't have a good idea of who yet or why. And that is puzzling. Usually, by this time and as deep into the research that we are, we should have an idea of who and why." Emma was puzzled by that.

"There are two sets of people after us, aren't there, Emma? I wish that I could work on it and see what I could come up with. My days are going to be very boring for now." Cullea regretted quitting her work but knew that she had made the right decision.

———

"I'm sure that you do." Emma paused as Abe slid over a note. "Listen. I can get the material to you tomorrow, if you like. Abe will send a couple of his guys and their ladies to meet with you."

"He would? Oh, that would be wonderful. I would like to help solve this and solve this soon. I want to get on with my life and so does Caleb."

"I am sure that he does. We'll get there, Cullea. The information sometimes just trickles in and then floods in at the end. Sometimes it floods in at the beginning and sometimes part way through. It is how God chooses to work that we need to wait for. He is our Defender, Cullea, in all ways. Sometimes we don't like what we go through and don't see that. Even if it means our death, He does defend us."

"I am beginning to understand that more and more. Thank you, Emma. You have helped."

"It's no problem, Cullea. Abe and I and all our guys went through stuff as did our ladies. So did many friends here and in Elmton. Talk to them. Caleb can give you their names. In fact, Toryn has a lady he knows who went through a lot. They thought for years that they were cousins. Only they weren't. She's married to the police chief in Elmton. Caleb knows them. They would be more than happy to talk with you."

"Thank you once more, Emma. I may reach out to them." Cullea dropped her phone back into her purse, lost in thought. She reached absentmindedly for her mug of tea, sipping at it and then just sitting and holding it. She had a lot to be thankful for and a lot to worry about.

Caleb stood in the hallway, watching his lady, his heart on his face. Ben had reached out to him just as he walked in his front door. He had finished his part of the training early and had headed home to shower and change before finding his lady. Caleb had not expected to hear that she was hiding at Ben's and that Ben felt he should head that way to find her. She needed him, did Caleb know and understand that? Ben took an interest in all of Don's men, Paul drawing them into his circle of friends. Paul had been brought into Ben's life when Ben found him on the streets and sick.

Chapter 25

Caleb walked forward to crouch beside his lady, his arms around her and a kiss planted on her temple. Cullea had jumped as she felt him hug her and then relaxed against him. How he had known to appear there, she wasn't sure. She was just glad that he did.

"Cullea? Sweetheart? Are you okay? Ben called me. He was worried when you showed up here." Caleb kept his voice calm despite the worry that flooded through his mind and heart.

"I am. I quit my work today, Caleb. I couldn't put them at risk, not any more. And then I could hear someone following me. I didn't look around to see how it was. When I came in here, Ben sent me to his office. I know that he's been hovering around in the hallway off and on." She turned her head to find herself nose to nose with Caleb.

"He called me. He just said that you were here and that I needed to be here as well." Caleb gathered her into his arms and sat back down in her chair, drawing a protest from her. "It's okay, sweetheart. It's okay. You need this."

Cullea stared at him before she nodded, her head going down against him. A finger rubbed at the button on his plaid shirt.

"I guess that I do. You make me feel safe and cherished." Cullea grew quiet, ashamed that she had spoken like that.

"I'm glad, sweetheart. That's what I want to do for you." Caleb studied the wall across from him, biting at his lip. "This is hard, you know. I want to keep you safe and can't. Your parents are gone again and you're on your own."

"I know. I spoke with Emma just now. She's sending someone over with stuff for me tomorrow. And you are at work."

"Tomorrow? No, I'm not training. I have maintenance to do on the work vehicles. You could come and keep me company." He waited for her to respond, letting her make her own decisions. He would back her in them unless she was in grave danger. That would change how he reacted and how his team reacted. Caleb knew that his team supported him in his decisions. They would only step in and take over if they had to.

"I could? I'll see. It's the evenings and nights that I worry about. They have proven that they will break into my house. I know the doors have been changed to steel doors. But even that wouldn't give me time to get away." Cullea worried about that and knew that her parents were as well.

"Cullea, I am going to ask you something, something that we should wait to consider. I love you. You love me. Will you marry me? Become my sweetheart for real? That way, we could be together when neither of us is at work." Caleb had put himself and his heart out there. He waited patiently for Cullea to respond, praying for his lady as he did so.

Cullea's movements stilled and it almost seemed as if she had stopped breathing. She had dreamed of a knight riding in and saving her from danger. But those had been dreams. This was real life. Was Caleb offering to be her knight and rescue her from danger? Only she knew that in doing so he was putting himself right in the line of fire. And no one could yet tell them which one of them was in danger. She was convinced it was herself. Caleb thought otherwise given that he worked in security.

"Do you mean that, Caleb?" Cullea's head went up as she studied the man holding her. She waited for him to bite at his lip and then nod, his eyes finding her. "Then, I accept. I agree. We should wait and get to know one another better. But this danger has proven otherwise."

Caleb reached to kiss her, his arms around the lady who he loved more than anything. It was not how he had expected to find his lady but given that was how his friends had, he should have known better.

"We'll make plans, sweetheart. How be we get together with our parents this weekend? It's only a couple of days away. We can make plans then."

"That would work. Mom and Dad will be back on Friday night." Cullea snuggled down against him, waiting for him to speak. She was not surprised that he began to pray instead. That was the character of the man who she loved.

Ben walked in at that point, his keen eyes studying the young couple. He nodded, knowing that they had reached an agreement. He could see a wedding between them in the near future. He sat down the tray that he carried on a table in front of them and then sat at his desk. Ben had paperwork to do but for now, he just prayed for his friends.

"Thank you, Ben. I don't understand how you know what we want or need." Caleb grinned at his friend.

Ben shrugged. He didn't know himself other than it was God. A good friend of his in Riverville was the same way. Mac could remember what a person ordered and provide it for them the next time that they were in his diner. They both maintained that this was how God worked through them.

"Eat up, Caleb. And then get your lady home. She hasn't been sleeping, I can tell." Ben bent his head over his paperwork, looking up every once in a while to watch the couple.

Cullea had stared at him and then down at her meal. It was exactly what she wanted. A grilled cheese sandwich and fries sat in front of her. A cheeseburger plate sat in front of Caleb. Caleb bowed his head, asked a blessing on their food and then began to eat.

Cullea finished her meal, forgetting that she was still sitting on Caleb's knee. She stood at last, gathering up the debris from their meal onto the tray, and heading for the kitchen. She felt safe now that Caleb was there.

Ben looked towards the door and then at Caleb, finding the younger man just sitting there, his eyes on his clasped hands. He sighed and prayed once more for the young man.

———

"Caleb? You're troubled." Ben spoke quietly, knowing that staff was moving back and forth in the hallway. He could faintly hear Cullea speaking with someone in the kitchen.

"I am, Ben. I am. I worry about Cullea. She quit her work today, something that she loved, just because she didn't want to bring harm to anyone. That's her character." Caleb was troubled and saddened by that.

"And she would be. She will have prayed it through, Caleb. We both know that." Ben rose and came to sit beside Caleb, a hand resting on his shoulder. "I sense that you two have made a decision. Let me pray with you for now. Then, you need to get your lady to her home."

Caleb nodded, a sober yet stern look on his face. Ben was right. They had made a decision, right or wrong, and he did need to get Cullea to her home.

———

Chapter 26

Saturday found the couple at Calum and Caiti's home. They had appeared there shortly after breakfast, causing the older couple to frown at them. Cullea's parents appeared not long after them, having let the younger couple leave on their own from Cullea's home.

Both sets of parents exchanged glances. Something had changed with the younger couple. The fathers shrugged, knowing that they would be told when the time was right. The mothers, however, were determined to find out what was going on.

Casee approached her daughter as she stood and leaned against the granite counter in the kitchen. With an arm around Cullea, Casee watched the emotions crossing her face. Caleb stood beside her, Cullea's hand tight in his.

"Cullea? What is going on? You asked to meet with us all this weekend. Now explain, young lady."

Cullea grinned at her mother. This had been a common phrase when Cullea was a teenager.

"We will, Mom. We will. We need everyone to gather together." Caleb's hand tightened on hers as she spoke.

"We do, Casee. How be we take our coffee and tea and the plate of scones and muffins and head for the sun room." He reached to fill trays, Cullea working with him.

Casee moved away, turning to watch her daughter and finding Caleb reaching to kiss Cullea. Something had changed with them. She felt Cowan's arm around her.

"They're in love, sweetheart." Cowan kept his voice low.

"They are. I think that they have come to an understanding." Casee turned in her husband's arms, welcoming his hug.

"I would suspect that we'll have a wedding and soon. It's not how we wanted to see this but it is what it is. God is leading them."

Calum set his mug aside on a nearby table. The younger couple had brought them up to date as much as they could. Calum was deeply worried about them but he agreed when they said they didn't know who or why. He had a name that he suspected was involved and had just passed it on to both Aidan and Don. They would work through it. He had also reached out to his friend in Mistletoe. Samuel Blackwell would help and he had promised that his son, Levi or Blackie as he was known as, would also look into it. There seemed to be something familiar about it all, Samuel had simply stated. Calum could almost guarantee that Blackie's three friends and all their wives would weigh in. That was how that group worked. It was the same with Caleb's team. They were working away to solve it but they just didn't have the information that they needed.

Raising their heads after a time to study the couple, the parents waited patiently. Caleb reached for Cullea's hand, his fingers touching the ring that he had just slipped back on her finger. They frowned at Caleb before frowning at Cullea.

"Mom. Dad. Cowan. Casee. Cullea and I have become engaged. We love each other. We are not willing to have a long engagement. Cullea and I have talked. We want to marry soon." Caleb kept his eyes on Cullea who was watching him in turn.

There was silence for a few moments. The parents had expected this but not so soon. Casee moved to sit beside her daughter, an arm around her.

"You're sure, Cullea?" Her mother's voice held love but also concern.

"We are, Mom. We want whatever time God gives us, whether it's long or short. Besides, being together will help to keep us safe. Or at least we hope it will."

"Okay, then." Calum spoke up then. "I know your heart, son. You will have prayed this through. When were you thinking?"

"Tomorrow? We have the license. Cullea has found her dress. We've spoken with Gideon. We don't want a huge wedding. Just you and our friends." Caleb sighed at that. "And that friend list is so huge."

Caiti began to laugh at that, causing Calum to laugh as well.

"You gather friends, son, and have a large group. Pick the ones that you really want there. Your team. Richard's team. Aidan. Toryn, Kaelen. Abe's team. Cullea? Your friends?"

Cullea was almost in tears. She didn't have friends in Oak City other than those who were friends with Caleb.

"I'm sorry. I don't know who I can ask." Cullea buried her head against Caleb, trying to stifle her sobs. Her mother's hand rested on her back. "I'm too dangerous to know right now."

"You have friends, sweetheart. You have Daci, Payten, and Taran. There are the two ladies on Richard's team and the men's wives as well. And then there are the eight ladies on Abe's team. They have reached out to you, I know. They want to be friends with you."

Cullea nodded, still not content that she had anyone to ask. She sighed to herself. *Lord, what do I do? How do I accept this fact and move on?*

"Don't worry, Cullea. They all feel that you're their friend. I can send out a text message to them all and they will be here. That's what we do for one another. And Daci, Payten, and Taran want to help you as well." Caleb shot a look up at Casee, finding compassion on her face even as she nodded.

"Let's make our plans, Cullea. Caleb, you know what you need to do." Caiti grinned at her son. "And a meal?"

"Ben will do that. He called me this morning, somehow knowing that we had reached a decision. He'll cater a cold meal for us, he said."

"That's good. Okay, then, we men will disappear for now. Caleb, you'll need to finish off what you need to do. We'll stop and talk with Ben as well. You ladies have planning to do." Calum was on his feet, heading for the door. He stopped as he stepped outside, watching as Daci, Payten, and Taran walked towards him. "How did you ladies know to come?"

"God, Calum. God told us that we needed to be here." Daci hugged Calum, having found him to be a father figure in her life when she needed one.

Chapter 28

A week later, Don walked towards Caleb's home. He held a large envelope in his hand. Don had found it on his front porch that morning. It was addressed to both Caleb and Cullea. He hadn't liked that it was there. Don had a bad feeling about it and that it meant more danger for the couple.

Caleb turned from the door, pointing towards the kitchen. He could hear Cullea singing to herself as she cleaned up after their breakfast. He was worried that Don was there on a Saturday and so early.

"Don? You're here and so early." Caleb reached to hug his bride.

"I am. I found this on the front porch this morning. It was delivered there although it is addressed to you two." Don handed the envelope to Caleb. "It should have come here."

"They want to keep the team involved." Caleb sighed as he set the table down. "Is Aidan on call this weekend?"

"He is. I'll call him." Cullea moved away to find her phone. She had thought that their adventure would heat up once they were married. She knew that God was in control but she still was very afraid.

Aidan turned from the crime scene where he had just finished what he needed to do. His phone out, he read Cullea's test. This was what he had been expecting. He sighed. There were just too many investigations on the go and this was just starting to ramp up for Cullea and Caleb.

Aidan reached for the envelope with his gloved hands. Caleb had handed it to him, knowing that Aidan would want to open it.

"This just appeared on your porch, Don?"

"It did, Aidan. It wasn't there late last night when I made the rounds outside. It was there early this morning. I checked my video feed after I found it. I couldn't make out much more than a dark shape. They avoided looking at the cameras. I would suspect that they have already cased the place and found out where they are."

Aidan's hand stilled. It was becoming clear to him that the people involved knew Don and his team and also Don's property.

"They've been around on a legitimate purpose and been able to move around freely. That means it is someone you know or who has been in for training."

"That's the conclusion we have come to. I have forwarded all the names of the trainees on to Emma. She has someone looking into them. As to the people I know? There are so many, Aidan. It's the same with all my guys. We have people we know in and out all the time, usually at the office building. There are some who do come around the house." Don was at a loss to explain who it might have been. There was a fear that he was trying hard to ignore that he was somehow responsible for all of what had happened.

"We'll get the names from you, Don, and look into them." Aidan turned his attention to the envelope. He studied it and then opened it. He peeked inside and then dumped out the contents. He was truly puzzled by them.

Caleb looked with interest at the objects before he frowned. The objects just didn't make sense. He could feel Cullea leaning against him, her hand finding his.

"What are these?" Cullea finally broke the silence.

Don studied them, a frown on his own face. He shared the thoughts of the others that the objects were bizarre.

"A square nail. An old postcard of a train station. A bird feather. A ruler. And a card." Aidan named the objects before his pen was out to open the card. "A sympathy card. Addressed to both Cullea and Caleb. It just says sympathy and nothing more."

"This is so strange, Aidan. What do they mean?"

"A ruler is used in building as is the nail. That would mean an old building when they used square nails. And the bird feather? It's red so I would suspect a cardinal. It is said that cardinals appear and remind you of a loved one. The sympathy card? I would suspect that they mean the death of either Caleb or myself." Cullea's voice was calm and collected. She felt that now maybe they could start to move forward in their search.

"That's all true, Cullea. I think that you have determined what they want. Now to find that old building."

"A barn? There are lots of old barns out there. Some abandoned and some in good shape. We would need to really search for them. Unless you two know of one." Aidan looked between Caleb and Don.

"I'm sure that we can come up with a list for you, Aidan. Just give us a couple of days. I'll reach out to others as well. Toryn may know of some as well. Kaelen would be a good resource. He flies over the area on a regular basis."

"That he does." Aidan snapped his fingers. "I'll find a time to go up with him and we'll search from the air. Now, if there's nothing else, I'll take all this and run." He waited as both Don and Caleb took photos of everything before he sealed it into evidence bags and then walked away.

Cullea was puzzled by what had appeared in the envelope. None of it really made sense, did it? She turned and walked away, leaving Don and Caleb speaking in the kitchen. Caleb watched her go, wanting to go with her but knowing that she needed some solitude.

"Caleb? How are you two really doing? We didn't get a chance to check in this Friday as we normally do. It was too hectic. We need to do better." Don felt remiss in that. He kept his team in his prayers and regularly checked in on how they were.

Caleb shrugged, not certain how to respond. He had found footsteps around the house that had appeared overnight and knew that house was being monitored on a daily basis if not more regularly.

"I don't know what to say, Don. So far, we haven't had any run-ins with anyone or faced abductions. We're trying to adjust to living with one another and that takes time. Cullea is at loose ends for now, not wanting to work in case that she brings danger to her co-workers. She's getting restless and wanting to be out." Caleb worried about her.

"If she is willing to do some office work, bring her with you on Monday. We'll set her up in the office and she can work through that. The other two ladies will certainly work with her and so will Daci." Don was on his feet. He had a lunch meeting that he needed to be at. "Stay safe, Caleb. You know well what to watch for. But sometimes we know something so well, we become less vigilant. Don't do that."

Caleb locked the door behind him, leaning against it for a moment. He headed after Cullea, finding her sitting on the side of their bed, not looking at anything. He sat beside her, an arm around her and simply prayed. God was there with them, he had no doubt. It was just hard to trust at times.

Chapter 29

Cullea had settled into a new routine, that of a housewife, but was not content with just that. She wanted to be a productive member of society. Yet, neither she nor Caleb was content with her working out in the community. They were seeing increasing signs of men moving around their home. They both worried about the other when they were apart.

That day, Cullea stared at the clock. It was only mid-morning and she desperately needed to get out of the house. She grabbed for her purse and her keys and locked up after herself. Her car was in the driveway and she headed that way. Driving away, she didn't see the truck that was following her, pulling away from the curb as she backed out of the driveway.

Wandering through the grocery store, Cullea tried to think of everything that she needed to purchase. She just couldn't and decided that it really didn't matter. It would give her something to do on another day.

Hearing her name called, Cullea looked around, her face lighting up as she saw Daci.

"I thought that you were working today." Cullea reached to hug the other lady.

"I am. I'm on a break and just decided to grab some stuff for the shelter. I see that you've escaped from the house."

"I did. I'm not sure that I should have but I did. Caleb will be worried if he knew." Cullea chewed at her lower lip, a new habit that Daci noted.

"He'll be fine with it. Just let him know where you are and if needed, he'll come and find you or one of the other guys will. If you need someone to go with you, Aidan has a lineup waiting to be asked. Don's team is well liked by our police force and works well with them. That's not true of all security teams. And if needed, Richard's team or friends and Abe's team and their friends will help."

"That's a lot of people, Daci. And I know that they did face difficulties. I've heard their stories. But you need to shop." Cullea shivered as she felt eyes on her and turned slightly, finding herself watched by a youth. "Do you know that youth over there?"

Daci had been facing that way and then nodded.

"I do. It's one of our police recruits. He's on duty with you today. He was likely waiting outside your home and then followed you. He'll have been in touch with Aidan who would have let Caleb know. Never be afraid to let Caleb or one of the guys know where you are. They would rather you bothered them with that than to have you disappear on them." Daci finished loading her cart with what she needed. "Now, what were your plans for the rest of the day?"

Cullea shrugged. She didn't know herself what she planned, so how could she tell someone else?

"I have no plans, Daci. I am so used to working that I don't know what to do with my free time."

———

"Then, come with me. We could use another volunteer in the office at the shelter. I know you have been helping out with Don's work. And he so appreciates that. The other ladies are taking turns as well. That means that he's not there for all hours after the team leaves doing paperwork. And another eye on the teams applying for training is helping. We ladies can sense when something is off." Daci simply grinned at her friend.

"We can, can we?" Cullea wasn't sure about that. Her ankle was aching that day, and she felt defeated and frustrated. "I just want this over, Daci. Caleb regrets our marrying as we did. He wanted to court me, he tells me."

Daci snorted at that, knowing that other friends had done the same thing.

"He can still court you. A friend from Riverville tells the men that if they marry quickly to just make their courting lifelong. It's how it should be." Daci paused as she shoved her groceries into her car. "So, will you come with me? We can head back to your place, put away your shopping, and then head for the shelter, Daniel will follow us."

Cullea shot a look at the young man who nodded at her and then at Daci. She shrugged once more, this time a smile briefly appearing on her face.

"I guess. It will help put in time. I just don't want to put the ladies at risk."

"They already are at risk, Cullea. They have all escaped from domestic violence. They understand what it's like to be afraid and to fear for their lives."

Working quickly, Cullea stuffed away her groceries and then locked up her home. She was off to do something new. An excitement began to rise within her. She felt like one of those victims and wanted to defeat whoever it was that was chasing her and chasing Caleb. Cullea just wished that they had more information as to who and why and could stop their adventure before anyone was hurt worse than they had been.

Caleb pulled out his phone shortly after that, his smile creasing his face. *Good*, he thought, *Cullea is getting out of the house. I worry about her staying home and I worry about her being out. I know that Aidan has arranged for someone to watch out for her and to follow her. Thank you, Daci, for giving her something to do. I pray for her safety and worry about her, but I have to leave it in Your hands, God. I can't be with her all the time. And experience has taught me that even if I am, things can still happen.*

Thomas had approached Caleb, leaning against the wall in the gym. His eyes were on the trainees as they went through their paces under the guidance of Paul and Joshua. He didn't speak at first, waiting for Caleb to do so.

"Caleb? Everything's okay with Cullea?"

"It is. Daci met her in the grocery store and has taken her to the shelter, ostensively to see how it works. Cullea needs that content with the ladies. She's feeling isolated and I don't know how to fix that."

"As much as we want to and try to, we can't fix how they feel. All we can do is to be there when they need us. Hold them when they cry. Take the anger that they throw out, not at us but at the situation. Hug them to help them feel better. Bring them flowers and whatnot to show our love for them. Pray for them and lead them to find the verses that will help." Thomas thought back over his adventure with Taran and realized that what he said was what he had tried to do.

"I get that, Thomas. It's just frustrating for her to be at home most of the time. She's not used to that. She's used to being out working and making a difference in others' lives."

"All our ladies are. Say, how about you and Cullea come for a meal one night this week? Paul and Payten are available as well. It might help."

"It would. Thanks, Thomas. I'll find out what day works for all of us." Caleb walked away at that point, not seeing Aidan who had entered the building, looking for him.

Aidan paused beside Thomas, a frown on his face. Something was off in there, he decided.

"Thomas? What is off in here? Something is." Aidan spoke quietly, not wanting to alarm anyone.

Thomas shot him a look and then nodded. He had felt something but hadn't been sure if it was in the building or not. He approached Don who shot a look towards Aidan and then moved to clear the building. This was what they had been expecting and prayed didn't happen.

Caleb ran for the house the next day, dodging the heavy raindrops. The clouds had opened up just as he pulled into the driveway. Unlocking the door, he stepped inside before he locked it behind him. His shoes were off and on the boot trap and his jacket hung in the closet. Caleb walked the house, searching for Cullea and not finding her. He frowned. Cullea had been adamant when they spoke at noon that she would be at home. And now she wasn't. His phone was out as he checked his messages. There was not a one from her.

Standing in the kitchen, his hand rested on the top of his head. Caleb became deeply worried. It was not like Cullea to be somewhere and then not be. He had come to depend on her reliability.

Heading for the office, Caleb sat at his desk, desperately praying for his wife. He was afraid that she had disappeared and that he would never find her. He found the video feed from noon on and watched on. He paused at the mid-afternoon, seeing the men at the door. Cullea had been out on the front porch, working with the flowers. She had not had time to run inside and lock the door. He could only watch as she struggled to release herself from their grips and being unable to do so.

Caleb's head bowed. What he had most feared had happened. Cullea had been taken from their home and while he was not at home. His phone out, he turned it over and over, not sure who to call.

"Aidan? It's Caleb." Caleb could hear the sounds of traffic coming through the phone. "I need you. "

Aidan paused before he turned his car and headed for Caleb. He suspected that Cullea had disappeared. The officer watching her had disappeared as well and no one had heard from him that afternoon.

"Caleb? It's Cullea?" Aidan prayed that his suspicions were wrong.

"It is. She was taken mid-afternoon, from the front porch. She was working away out there with the flowers. She didn't have a chance." Caleb drew in a shaking breath. "I have the video feed pulled up."

"And with the rain, we won't get much. Call Don or one of your team. And call both sets or parents. Have them stay away until we can see what we can retrieve. Have Don or one of the guys with you." Aidan threw his phone on the passenger seat. This was not to have happened.

Don watched Caleb as he paced his kitchen. Aidan and a crime scene tech were in his office watching the video feed. The other four men on the team were around, speaking with their neighbours on their own or watching the work around the house.

"Caleb? Talk to me. When did you talk with Cullea last?" Don spoke at last, bringing Caleb's attention to him.

"At lunch. You know we had a late lunch just because of this morning. It was around one, I think. Somewhere in that time frame. And I was home just after four. The video feed shows it happened around 2:30. They've been watching us that closely."

"They have been. And the area outside is searched every day. Your vehicles are searched before you leave and when you leave to come home." Don was frustrated at that. "Did you call your parents?"

"I did. They're horrified. They want to be here but Aidan doesn't want any more people in and out of the house until they're finished. I just don't understand why." Caleb turned away, heading for his bedroom and his Bible. He needed that time alone, just to sit in God's presence and try to find peace about the situation. He would also petition the heavens for his lady to come home and come home that night.

Don pulled out his phone and squinted at the number.

"Emma? You're calling?"

"I am. We're on Caleb's street but can't get near the house. Which one?" Emma's voice held her worry, something that Don knew very seldom happened.

"Cullea. She disappeared this afternoon. It was caught on their security system. Caleb found her gone when he arrived home just after four."

"That's what I was so worried about. Once we can get through, we need to meet with both you and Caleb. We have information that may help. We've sent it on to Aidan as well."

Abe shook his head as he listened to Emma's conversation with Don. It was what they had expected but had prayed would not happen. He needed to take with both Don and his team. His heart went out to Caleb, knowing how devastating it could be to have this happen.

"We need to wait, Abe." Emma pulled out her phone, working away as she waited. She was not one to sit still if an investigation was in the process of being worked on.

"I guess. Where's Richard today?"

"Richard? I think this is the week that he and Raleigh were away. He would be here if he could be."

"I know." Abe's fingers tapped on the steering wheel. He was running scenarios, trying to come up with a plan to discuss with Don. "This is where it gets hard for them. They don't have much information, do they?"

"They didn't. What Evan, Jace, and I found will help. It should push the investigation forward. No one will believe the names that we have found."

"And you have the proof that you need. All of you are like that. You don't make accusations without it." Abe started his truck and pulled up to park in front of Caleb's home. The police vehicles had mostly left, only one patrol car parked in the driveway to provide protection.

Don walked towards Abe, feeling the chill in the air now that the rain had stopped. He just prayed that Cullea was under cover and safe wherever she was.

______

"Abe? I didn't expect to see you here today." Don reached to hug Emma. "You have information for us."

"I do. And here are the parents." Emma moved away to greet the ladies, her hugs a little bit longer than normal. She then walked towards the house with Caiti and Casee.

Calum and Cowan waited with Don and Abe, not sure what they should be doing. They only knew that they had to do something.

"Fellows? What do you know?" Cowan broke the silence at last. He still heard the sobs in Caleb's voice as he told him that Cullea had disappeared and the sobs that his wife had uttered as he held her.

"Cullea disappeared mid-afternoon. We'll take a look at the video feed." Abe looked past Calum. "Calum? This man seems to be looking for you?"

Calum turned before he walked rapidly towards the man. He had not expected Samuel and Blackie to show up, but he should have. That must mean that they too had information for them.

"Let's get inside, fellows." Don walked that way, hesitation in his steps for a moment. He waved his team towards the house. The two wives were there as was Daci, wanting to help but not sure how they could.

Chapter 31

Caleb listened to the conversation going on around him. His thoughts were centred on his bride and where she was. His heart was breaking. He wanted Cullea with him and she wasn't. Calum watched his son closely, his own heart breaking for his son. This was one time that he could not fix the matter or make it all better for his son.

Don stood for a moment, heading for the outdoors. He needed some space to think through what he had been told. The name that Emma had come up with? It had been totally unexpected at the time but thinking through it, he nodded. It made sick sense. He turned as he heard footsteps. Blackie stood beside him.

"Don? What can we do for you?" Blackie had shared the story of Julia, his wife, and him as well as the stories of his three friends.

"I'm not sure, Blackie. I can't thank you and your Dad enough for what you have discovered. It is helping to make sense of all of this." Don was at a loss, however, not sure where they went.

"It is difficult, I know. Caleb will need all the support that you can give him. I've spoken with both Paul and Thomas. They will help him the most, having gone through what they did. No one can truly understand how another person feels and it is wrong to say that we do. God is in the midst of this, Don. This is when it gets so hard to trust. All we can do at the present is pray for Cullea and that God protects and defends her. She will come home."

"And I hear what you're not saying. We may not like the condition in which she returns." Don's eyes were on Calum and Cowan who had come to find him. He saw the understanding in their eyes.

"You might not. It's really hard to just wait and trust that God is in control. We will continue to pray for you and your team and particularly for Caleb and Cullea. If you need us, do not hesitate to contact us." Blackie and Samuel walked away, heading for home.

The two fathers approached Don at that point. Abe had wandered out to join them, knowing that as a team leader, Don felt a lot of responsibility for his team. He didn't know what he could say that would help.

"Don, what can we do? I know that Blackie and Samuel will have left a lot of material that we need to go over. Neither one of us is working at present. Let us go over and see what we can find." Cowan spoke quietly and confidently, knowing that, while he was not an investigator, he could organize what was needed and work through it.

"Thanks, Cowan. That will help. I suggest that we meet at my office building in the morning. I know that the four of you won't leave here tonight. The ladies should be part of this. We can't leave them out of it."

"That we can't. Caleb needs us nearby. His mother won't leave him. Not while he is going through this. I just don't understand it." Calum rubbed at the back of his neck, not sure what his son was facing other than having his bride disappear.

———

"Caleb does need us all. We'll go through what Samuel left, what Emma has found, and what we have found. We'll combine it all and see what we find. We have names that we need to look into further." Don walked away, heading for his home but not to sleep. He spent the night in intercession for his friend and his bride.

The next morning, Don watched as his team gathered in the conference room. He knew the wives were here and in his kitchen as were the two sets of parents. Caleb was moving very slowly that morning, his grief and worry uppermost and evident to all.

Mark paused beside Don, his own eyes assessing Caleb. He shook his head. This was not what Caleb should be going through, not as a newlywed.

"Don, what do we do? How much information do we really have?" Mark kept his voice low, his eyes finding their team mates and then the ones who had joined them. He was not surprised to see Kaelen there.

"I think we have enough that we can start putting it all together. Let's spend some time in prayer first. Caleb and Cullea need it and so do we." Don moved to his chair, his hand resting on the back of it for a moment. He was uncertain what was coming but he feared for Cullea's life. She might not come back as they were praying.

Caleb raised his head at last and studied those with him. Joshua and Paul were seated on either side of him. He was afraid for his bride and worried beyond anything that he had ever been worried. He waited somewhat impatiently for Don to speak.

Don studied each person in the room. He nodded to himself. They were all gathered there to try and make sense of what information that they had.

"Okay, people. Let's start working through this. We'll go through it on our own, make our notes, and then combine them." Don watched as heads were bent over the papers, the sounds of shuffling paper and scratching pens the only sounds in the room.

Mark rose at that point and headed for the whiteboards. The ladies had been scribing down the comments, facts, and suppositions all morning. He traced the track through it and then turned, looking for Joshua. Joshua was on his feet and walking towards him even as Caleb approached Mark.

"Mark? What did you discover?" Caleb kept his voice low as he questioned his friend.

"This! This name! He's approached us many times but we always turned him away. He wanted to be part of our team and he wasn't a good fit. Don always refused. Now, you tell me. Is he going after you or after Don? He is a mechanic, Caleb, so he may be trying to take you out of the team and then move into your place."

Caleb nodded. He knew the man that Mark was questioning. That man didn't have a good reputation in town and everyone knew it.

"It could be both. Why don't we ask Emma to look into him if she isn't already? I have a feeling that he goes a lot deeper than me." Caleb walked away, heading for the outdoors. He needed some space and only outside would do. He stood for a moment in the shadow of the building before he walked away and headed for his truck. He stopped beside it, a hand on the door handle before he reached for the envelope tucked under a wiper blade. Caleb stared at it before he looked around and then headed back for the building. Someone had been there and he wanted to know who.

Mark looked around, surprised to see Caleb walking towards him. He saw the anger on his friend's face and froze for a moment. Caleb simply pointed back out of the conference room and then headed for Mark's office.

"Caleb? Didn't you just leave?" Mark sat at his desk, not sure what was going on. He only knew that his friend was angry and was also waving an envelope at him.

"This It was on my truck. Who put it there?" Caleb's question drew Mark's eyes to his before Mark nodded and was reaching for his computer mouse, ready to pull up the security feed.

Chapter 32

Caleb waited somewhat impatiently as Mark worked through his security protocol and then began a search. He didn't think that Mark would find anything good about the man. He stared down at the envelope. The long white envelope had his name printed on it and not by hand. Someone had printed the envelope from a computer program. That told him that they were going to extremes to hide their identity.

Opening it, Caleb pulled out the folded piece of paper. He knew that once he unfolded it, there would be no going back. He sighed to himself and then began to pray. He knew the verses that would be quoted at him if he were to ask. He knew the counselling that Gideon, their pastor, would offer, the same that his father and Cullea's father would offer. He didn't want that. Caleb just wanted his bride back beside him. And that didn't seem possible at the moment.

Mark looked up at that point, his mouth open to speak with Caleb. He snapped it shut, waiting instead for Caleb to read his letter and then respond.

Caleb unfolded the letter, seeing that it too was printed from a computer. That wasn't much help for him, he decided, knowing that it would be difficult if not impossible to determine the computer. That was, unless the computer was found and searched and the letter showed up in the trash bin or in the computer history.

His eyes dropped to the words and his heart fell. He was not prepared for what it said. He read it multiple times before his hand dropped to his lap and he just sat and stared at the floor. Caleb's thoughts were muddled and angry and distraught and hurting.

Mark rose, seeing the look on Caleb's face and came around his desk. Gently, he reached to retrieve the letter from Caleb's hand and turned as he heard footsteps. Aidan stood in the doorway, having arrived just to check in with the group. He had not expected to find Caleb in the shape that he was.

"Mark? What's going on?" Aidan entered the office, closing the door behind him. His instincts told him that something drastic had just happened.

"Caleb found this on his windshield just a bit ago. I just read it. It's brutal, Aidan." Mark handed it over to the detective, handling it carefully.

Aidan motioned for him to drop it to the top of the desk even as he reached for gloves that he snapped on his hands. His eyes were on Caleb for a moment, assessing the other man. It can't be good, he decided, before he read the letter.

We have your lady. She is not coming home. She is now working for us. Too bad. So sad. You had your chance and blew it. Now, your life is forfeit as well.

Aidan drew in a deep breath. There was no way that Cullea would work for a criminal organization. Of that he was certain. He gathered up the letter and the envelope, nodding as Mark asked to take a photo of it. He was away, heading for the office and Toryn. His own supervisor needed to be in on that conversation.

This was hurting friends of theirs and it needed to stop and stop then.

Calum stood in the office doorway, having come to find his son. There were questions that they needed to ask him. He sat beside Caleb, an arm along his son's shoulders. Caleb didn't move and didn't respond to his father's voice.

"Mark? What happened? Something did."

"It did. Caleb found a letter on his windshield." Mark handed over his phone, seeing the distress and anger that flickered across Calum's face.

"They said this? It's brutal, Mark. So, how do we find them?" Calum was determined to find the ones responsible and find them that day.

"We search, Calum. Caleb and I came up with a name. Teddy Allen." Mark waited for Calum to respond.

"Teddy Allen? He's involved? Of course, he is. And his brother, Todd, and his cousin, Dustin. They have always been on the wrong side of the law. He wanted to take over Caleb's place, Caleb thought."

"He did. He tried it a few years ago and Don sent him packing. This is his revenge on Caleb. He's never been able to keep a girlfriend for more than a day. All the young ladies in town who are our ages avoid him like the plague."

Calum grinned at that, knowing it was true, before he sobered. Now, it was all beginning to make sense. That was, except for Cullea's involvement. He turned as he heard Cowan entering the room. The two men didn't know that Cowan had heard their conversation.

"I heard what you said. How would Cullea be involved?" Cowan was thinking it through, trying to decide just what they would want from his daughter.

"She's an audiologist." Caleb looked up, devastation on his face. "If they could use hearing aids to direct people to steal or whatever, they would use her skills to do that, wouldn't they?"

The three men with him drew in deep breaths. Caleb had more than likely put his finger on why she was taken. They had to prove it and then find the evidence that was needed. All four men were on their feet, heading back for the conference room. Determination coloured their faces and their steps.

The occupants of the room looked around as they entered, Don on his feet to approach them. Something major had just happened, he could tell. He took the phone that Mark was thrusting at him and read the letter. His brows lowered as he read it. This is not what was needed, he knew, but they would work with what they had and solve it. Cullea needed to come home and Caleb needed his bride. That was not an option, not any more.

Joshua and Paul headed for the security room, ready to pull up the feed and discover who had been there. They stared at each other in shock at the person that appeared. It was a woman from their church, a girl actually in her late teens. How did she become involved?

———

Joshua's phone was out as he called Aidan. Aidan was shocked as well and simply asked for a copy of that portion of the security feed. He would bring that teen in and question her. Since she was over eighteen, he would not need to go through her parents, not yet anyway.

Chapter 33

Caleb paced his house that night, worry and discouragement uppermost. He had sent everyone home, not wanting to be around his family or friends. None of them had liked it but knew it was what he wanted. He didn't know that Mark and Joshua were parked right outside his home, taking turns keeping watch over him. It was what Caleb himself would have done.

Reaching for his Bible, Caleb sat in the chair that Cullea had favoured in their living room. He felt closer to her there. His eyes closed as he wept, praying for his bride and her safety. He had to finally release her to God's hands, knowing that if God so choose, she would not come home as he prayed that she would. He had to prepare himself for that eventuality.

Early morning found him tapping at the window of Mark's truck, waiting for Joshua to roll it down.

"Come on in, guys. I have breakfast ready for us. That is, if you want fresh coffee." He turned and walked back to his house.

Mark studied him before he frowned. Something was different about Caleb in the early morning light.

"He's discovered something, Mark." Joshua was out of the truck and walking after him, entering the kitchen to find Caleb dishing up their food. "Caleb?"

"We eat, Joshua Then we need to pray. I have an idea where she is. Dad called late last night and asked some hard questions. One of them got me thinking. I've been searching." Caleb squinted at the clock. It was only five in the morning. "It's early but the timing would be right to move in and find them."

"I'm sure you know what you're talking about." Mark reached to pour their coffees, thinking that it would likely be a long day.

"I will explain. I called Don earlier. He, Paul, and Thomas are heading for that area. We'll join them once we eaten and prayed." Caleb sat, his head bowing as Mark asked the blessing on their breakfast.

"It will go quicker if you talk as we eat, Caleb." Joshua was not backing down from his friend.

"Okay, this is what I discovered. I took the Allen names and began to research them. Jace reached out to me overnight. He gave me some addresses and I looked them up. I focused on one that is outside of town but still within our law enforcement jurisdiction. I suspect that they think they are out of our jurisdiction."

"I would suspect that as well." Mark rose to begin to clear away the remains of the meal. "When is Don going to be there?"

Caleb squinted at the clock and then nodded.

"He was to be there by 5:30. We should be there around the same time. It's only about ten minutes from here."

His two friends stared at him and then at one another. So close and yet so far, they thought. Lord, let us find Cullea and get her home today. They need one another and we need to solve this.

Heading for Mark's truck, Caleb searched his neighbourhood. He had felt watched the night before but not now. He figured it was too early for someone to be there. And that was just okay with him.

Mark headed for the road where the campground lay. He paused near the entrance and then pulled off into a small layabout to one side. His truck was hidden from the driveway. A few moments later, Don pulled in. None of the men in Mark's truck was surprised to see Aidan with them.

"Aidan's here? Does he have a search warrant?" Joshua reached to open his door, dropping to the ground and heading for his team leader. "Don?" He kept his voice low, knowing that it could sound loud in the early morning air.

"I brought Aidan in so that we have police involvement. Toryn arranged for search warrants for us. Let's pray and then move in." Don was as good as his word, his head bowed to lead them in prayer. This was a dangerous move, they all knew, and could mean harm to Cullea. A friend from the street had confirmed that Cullea was here. They just needed to move in and find her.

Aidan studied Caleb before he moved in on him, a hand out to stop him. Knowing Caleb, Aidan was certain that Caleb would want to be one of the men going in. He couldn't allow it, not at all. He and Toryn had discussed it and that had been their agreement.

"Caleb? I can't let you go onto the grounds. We need two of you to stay with the trucks." Aidan's voice and face held compassion and sympathy for Caleb. He was surprised when Caleb simply nodded.

"I figured that one out, Aidan. Mark has left me his keys. Don left Paul his. So we wait. Just find Cullea and bring her back to me. That's all I ask." Caleb struggled for a moment to control his emotions before he pointed towards the others. "Go on. Find them."

Don had turned to watch Caleb, not surprised to hear his words. It was the character of all his team to not stand in the way of justice or proper procedure. He nodded at Aidan as they quickly faded into the low light of the campgrounds, heading for one particular trailer. They approached it, the men circling around it to keep watch for anyone trying to escape.

Aidan hammered at the door, his voice calling out for the occupants to exit, that police were on scene. There was no response. His hand reached for the door and opened it, a hand up for Don to follow him. The two men quickly entered the trailer, a mobile home really, and began their search. The door to the bedroom opened slowly and quietly under Aidan's hand and he stopped for a moment.

His eyes searching the dim room, he found the person he was seeking. Don was beside him, scooping Cullea into his arms and then almost running from the trailer. Aidan followed quickly, his phone out to call in the personnel who were waiting down the road. Activity soon woke the residents who stood in the dawning light, not sure what had happened to their home area.

Caleb straightened up as he heard running footsteps and the team appeared. Don headed for him, Cullea in his arms. Caleb simply reached for his bride, cradling her to him, disturbed that she had not roused. Mark's hand on his back shoved him towards the truck where Joshua stood at the open back door. Inside, Caleb refused to let his bride go, desperate for her to awaken but knowing that she may be drugged.

Mark sped away, a police car leading him, heading for the hospital. Cullea was quickly transferred to a stretcher and wheeled inside. Caleb refused to leave her side, ignoring the commands of the medical personnel. Mark and Joshua planted themselves outside of her door, leaving Don, Paul and Thomas to head for the waiting room. Don's phone was out as he called the two sets of parents at Caleb's request.

Chapter 34

Cullea slowly roused, hearing sounds in her ears that she didn't recognize. It was not the voice of the man who had demanded and commanded that she work for him. He shouted at her to work for him and that she would never go home. If she tried to escape, her husband and family would be killed and killed in front of her. Cullea had shuddered at that and then shut down. He had not been able to get a response from her after that. His shouts had fallen on ears that did not hear or understand.

She felt a hand on her cheek and another holding her hand. She was puzzled, sure that it was Caleb, and dismayed that he too was a captive. She had prayed as hard as she could that he didn't join her, not like that.

"Cullea? Sweetheart? Open your beautiful eyes, sweetheart. We have you safe." Caleb bent close over the stretcher, his mouth near Cullea's ear. He waited for her to rouse, not leaving her side.

Her parents had been allowed in to see her and then asked to leave. Casee had not wanted to but knew that she had to. She sobbed quietly in Cowan's arms, her tears alarming those around her. Caiti moved to sit beside her, knowing how she had felt when Caleb had disappeared.

Her eyes opening at last, Cullea stared around, wonder on her face. She was no longer in that cramped mobile home, threatened hourly with her death and the deaths of her loved ones if she refused to work with the man. Cullea didn't know the man's name but she had seen him at the hospital. She frowned as memories flooded back. He had also been around her former work.

Her head turned as she heard a prayer whispering in her ear. Caleb was there, his forehead touching her temple as he prayed for her. An arm was around her and her one hand was clasped tightly in his. Caleb was not letting go of his beloved bride, not at that point anyway.

"Caleb?" Cullea had to clear her throat to speak. "Caleb? Are you all right?"

"Cullea? You're awake! Thank God you're home. I was so afraid for you." Caleb raised his head to study her beloved face before he kissed her. "We'll get you home soon, sweetheart."

"Thank you, Caleb. I think that I need to speak with someone." Cullea searched for the police officer or detective who she knew would be there. "Who is waiting for me?"

"Aidan is here. He was part of the team who went in and found you." Caleb turned as he heard the door open and then footsteps. "Here he is, sweetheart. I'll be right outside." Caleb reluctantly walked away from her.

Aidan watched him walk away before he turned back to Cullea. He found her staring at him, a determined look on her face.

"Cullea? We need to get your statement." Aidan dropped his briefcase on the bedside table. "I've asked the medical personnel to give us some time."

"I agree. You need to find that man, Aidan. He is a very dangerous and callous individual. I don't want to see anyone else fall into his hands. And that is exactly what I fear will happen."

"I pray that we can do just that, Cullea. Okay, now talk to me. We know when you disappeared. We just don't know who or why." Aidan's pen was ready as was his laptop to take her statement.

"I see. I thought that you would. It's difficult to state what happened. Now, to go back to that day. I was working around inside the house. It had seemed as if it had been a very long day. I knew that Caleb would be home just after four. He had told me that and also told me that we would go out for a meal, so I hadn't prepared anything for our supper.

"I heard the hammering and slamming at the front door and tried to find somewhere to hide. The front door was broken in just as someone ran through the back door. I hadn't locked it as I had been in and out on the back porch. I couldn't move as my feet felt frozen. I turned to try and run and that's when one of the men wrapped me into a hold and carried me out of the house. I fought, Aidan. I fought to get away and couldn't. His hold was just too tight. I was thrown into a car and then handcuffed. A gag was slapped across my mouth.

"They drove around for what seemed hours and I guess it was. They were waiting for dark to take me to that campground. I could hear them laughing amongst themselves. They were convinced that they were outside of your jurisdiction. I don't think that they were. It really wasn't that far outside of town.

"Anyway, they locked me into that bedroom after they removed the handcuffs and gag. I tried to get out but they had secured the windows in such as way that I couldn't. And I knew that someone was still out in the living area. I could hear them moving around and the occasional phone call.

"The next morning, that man appeared and they dragged me out to face him. I can work with a police artist on a sketch. His face is burned into my memory. He's an evil, vindictive man. He ordered me to work with him and was very angry when I refused. He just kept hammering his words at me, telling me that I would never go home and that Caleb and my family would never see me again. I was going to work for him and do what he ordered me to do. I kept refusing. They would do this every couple of hours, even during the night. If it wasn't him, then it was one of his men."

"What did he want you to do, Cullea?" Aidan waited patiently for her to compose herself once more.

"It was strange and bizarre, Aidan. He knew that I was an audiologist. He had some pan that I would be able to put in a microphone to a hearing aid and that he could then control whoever it was that was wearing it. It didn't make sense. I have never done that and have no desire to do it. He just kept telling me that was what I would do from now on." Cullea looked up at that point, devastation on her face. "If he did that, I don't know who he could have controlled. We need to stop him, Aidan."

"And we will. We'll work with you on a police sketch. We have an idea who he is. He's not really all that smart." He grinned as she snorted.

"I would suspect the trailer was either in his name or a family member's name. He didn't strike me as all that smart in any way. Thank you, Aidan." Cullea's eyes were having trouble staying open. "I didn't sleep the whole time. I don't know how you found me or saved me, but thank you." She slept and didn't hear Aidan's soft words.

"It wasn't me, Cullea. It was Caleb and Don. They're the ones who you need to thank." Aidan packed away his belongings, hesitating for a moment before he walked to open the door. He nodded at Caleb that he was finished with the statement and watched as Caleb rushed to be by Cullea again. His prayers were raising fervently and anxiously for his friends.

Chapter 35

Starting at Caleb, Cullea's face held defeat and shame. She told herself that she should not be defeated or feel shame. It wasn't working, that much was obvious. Caleb reached to draw her into his arms. He had brought her home not that long ago, long enough that she had cleaned up and was looking for something to eat. He held her, feeling the shudders running through her body.

"Caleb? How do we do this? How do we stay safe? I don't know that we are any more." Cullea's voice was muffled against him as his arms tightened around her.

"I don't know, sweetheart. I really don't know. Don and the team are meeting right now to come up with plans. Both Richard and Abe are in town to meet with them." Caleb sat her on the couch in the living room and was gone from the room, returning with the tray holding their simple meal. He set it on the coffee table and then wrapped her into his arms once more. He was afraid to let her go, sure that she would disappear on him once more.

Cullea nodded, waiting for him to pray. When he didn't, she turned her head to find him just staring at the wall across from him. She didn't think that he was concentrating on the cream walls or the painting of a forest in the autumn colours.

"Caleb? What are you thinking?" Cullea waited patiently for her groom to speak, knowing that he needed time to do so.

Caleb's thoughts came back to Cullea when she spoke. They had talked briefly about what happened and what Cullea had been asked to do. He was puzzled by it all. Instead of speaking to her, he began to pray. He was incredibly worried about her and knew that she was worried about him. How did they do this now? He had no ideas. Caleb prayed that this would be over soon and that they would both survive.

"I have no idea what to think, sweetheart. We're not done with that man as yet. It was strange what he asked of you." Caleb watched Cullea's face closely.

"It was. That isn't something that I can do. And if he finds someone, how would we ever stop him?" Cullea was struggling to understand it all.

"That's what I fear. We need to find what information we can and bring him down." Caleb handed her the plate that he had fixed for her. "Eat, sweetheart, and then you need to sleep."

Cullea nodded and then handed him back her plate. She wasn't hungry, just wanted to sleep. She turned to rest against him and did just that. Caleb watched her closely before he too slept. They didn't hear the commotion outside their home. Some of the men who had held Cullea were trying to enter once more. Only, this time the authorities were waiting for them. Struggles ensued before the men were down on the ground and handcuffed. They were hauled to their feet and then shoved into patrol vehicles. Aidan was there, watching closely before he turned to watch the house. He would be back later. At the moment, Aidan needed to be on another crime scene.

Cullea was on her feet three hours later, leaving Caleb still asleep on the couch. She covered him with a blanket and then walked away, heading for the kitchen and making fresh coffee. A mug of it in her hand, Cullea headed for the office. She was determined to end their adventure and end it that day. She was stretching, she knew, to do that. Cullea didn't think that they could do that but she would do her very best.

Caleb rose at last, squinting in the dark room. It was late evening and he didn't realize that he would sleep that long. He headed for the kitchen, finding the coffee still ready and poured a mug. He too headed for the office, pausing in the doorway to watch Cullea. She had papers spread out all over the place, her hair ruffled from running her hands through it. He simply walked over, set down his mug on the desk, and picked her up to sit in her chair.

Cullea jumped as she felt hands on her and then snuggled back against Caleb. He was here and now she could go over with him what she had found. She didn't understand it at all. Emma had reached out during the night, just praying for her. Her text message had meant a lot to Cullea.

"You've been busy, sweetheart." Caleb's forefinger poked at the piles of papers.

"I have been. I have discovered some things and some people but I'm not sure who or what they are." Cullea prayed that Caleb could make sense of it all. "Caleb? Where is God in all this?"

Caleb sat back in the chair, his arms tightening around his lady love. He studied her face, knowing that she was asking for a reason. It was more than likely the same reason that he was asking that.

"He's here, sweetheart. Right in the midst of all this. He never lets us go through a storm on our own. He protects and defends us against our enemies. God gives peace and calms us during these times. I have no doubt about that. He uses people like us to bring criminals to justice."

"I know that, Caleb. It's hard to trust at time. I guess that's where faith comes in." Cullea grew silent, her thoughts on the verses that she had been memorizing.

"That it is, sweetheart. Now, let's see what you've discovered. And I am sure that you have discovered something. Did you get any sleep at all?" Caleb watched her closely as she sighed.

"None. I couldn't. I don't know if I can until we end this. And I want it over now."

"We both do." Caleb reached for the top papers and read through them. He stacked them neatly to one side as he finished each one. He then reached for a pad of paper and pen and began to make his own notes on what he had read. Cullea watched him, an arm around his neck. She knew that she should move and sit in her own chair but being with Caleb like this? She felt loved and safe and cherished.

"What did you discover, Caleb?" Cullea reached to still his hand, reading what he had written. "Who are these people?"

———

"Someone high up in the college here. In the audiology program, no less." Caleb shifted his seat so that he could watch her face. He nodded his head. "Do you know him?"

"I've heard of him. Anyone in the area who works in the field has." Cullea grew silent, a frown on her face. "And it always hasn't been good. There are a number of rumours. But that doesn't explain you."

"No, it doesn't. My specialty is vehicles." Caleb could not understand why he had been abducted in the first place.

"That's why I don't understand. How do our occupations combine? Or do they?" Cullea reached to take the pen from his hand and turned to a new page of paper. "We need to think this through, Caleb."

Chapter 36

Don watched Caleb three days later. He was worried about him, not sure what was going on. Caleb had handed him the papers that he and Cullea had been working on, simply giving the man's name. Don had stared at him and then nodded. It was beginning to make sense. He just didn't know how that they would prove it.

Caleb turned from his computer that afternoon. He had been through the training with the team in as it related to vehicles and what they needed for their team and what to watch out for. He was exhausted, he decided, but not ready to quit. Rising, Caleb walked through the building, seeing that his team had all left. He sighed as he stared at his watch. He needed to leave. He wanted to find Cullea but wasn't sure that she wanted to see him.

Walking towards their front door, Cullea sighed to herself. She thought that she was sighing too much but life had her in its hard grip. No matter how much she begged and petitioned God, this was not ending or moving from her. She peeked out and saw Caleb standing there, hesitant to enter his own home. He had no idea why. He just wanted to be with his lady.

Caleb stared at her and then reached to wrap her into his arms. He was deeply afraid for her and just wanted to wrap her in his arms and not let go of her. He realized that he couldn't, not yet anyway. At least, he didn't think that he could.

Cullea moved away from him, her eyes on the scene outside the door. She reached for an envelope taped to the front area of their home. Caleb reached to take it from her, turning her and almost shoving her into the house. He slammed the door after her and locked it, his eyes on her.

"Caleb? What are you thinking?" Cullea stood in front of him, a woebegone look on her face for a moment.

"I am thinking that I love you deeply and don't want to lose you at all." Caleb reached to draw her to him, holding her close to his heart. "I wish that I could just marry you again and then run away with you until they find whoever it is."

"You would do that?" Cullea drew in a deep breath. He had just answered her prayer. She had been begging God to bring in someone to defend her and praying that it would be Caleb. "Then, why don't we? I mean, we are all ready married. I do love you too, Caleb."

Caleb stared down at her, shock for a moment in his heart before he kissed her. He held her tighter to him and then turned them to the room that she had set up as her office.

"We need to pray this over, sweetheart, and then plan. I hate that you had to miss out on anything that leads up to a wedding."

Cullea was frustrated and walked away from him to stand at the window for a moment. She turned back to find him standing and watching her. She walked back into his arms, her own around him.

"We're not getting anywhere with the investigation. Maybe if we take this next step, it will shake things up and bring whoever it is out into the open. If we run, then they might follow us" She pointed to the letter that he had dropped down on the desk. "What is in there?"

"I have no idea. I guess that we need to open it to find out. Only, I'm reluctant to." Caleb picked it up and stared at him before Cullea simply reached and took it from him.

Cullea opened the envelope and dropped the photos onto the desktop. She reached for a pen to move them around and then flip them over. There was no note or anything to say what it was all about.

Caleb wrapped an arm around her and studied the pictures. He was puzzled. They were not what he had expected.

"This is strange, Caleb. What does it mean? These pictures are not of us or our families. Nor even our friends. I don't know these people. Do you?" Cullea looked up at him when he didn't respond.

"I do, unfortunately, Cullea. These are the men that we are looking at being behind all this." He reached for his phone, took his photos, and then sent a text off to Aidan and then to Don. "Someone on our side left this for us."

"They did? I guess they did. These men wouldn't have sent them to us. Not at all." Cullea was content to be held, surprising herself. She usually shunned physical contact.

Caleb was puzzled as well, not sure what was happening. He knew that Aidan would appear when he could. He just didn't understand it at all.

The ringing of the doorbell roused the couple from their thoughts. Cullea turned towards the door, stopping as Caleb's hand went out. He instead headed for the door, peeked out and then opened it to see Don and his team there. The ladies were there as well. He could also see the two sets of parents heading their way. And bringing up the rear were Aidan and Kaelen.

Caleb simply pointed towards the office before he headed for the kitchen. Kaelen followed as did the two mothers. He squinted at the clock. It was past time for their dinner, but he wasn't sure if any of them felt like eating.

Aidan paused at the desk, his eyes on Cullea before they dropped to the desktop. He frowned before he reached out with his own pen to move them around and then flip them over. He knew the men and women in the photos but was not aware that they were suspects. He pulled on latex gloves and gathered them up and then tucked them into an evidence bag. Excusing himself, Aidan left, heading for the office and to speak with Toryn.

Cullea turned as she heard a voice asking her a question. She frowned at Mark before she walked away, needing to find some solitude. Only that didn't seem possible. Payten and Taran had followed her, knowing that she needed to be alone but that she also needed their support. They simply sat near her, praying for her as they did so.

Knowing that she had friends nearby, Cullea curled up a chair. Her thoughts were troubled. She was attempting to think through what had happened but Caleb's declaration of his love for her kept getting in the way.

"Cullea?" Payten waited patiently for Cullea to turn to her. "What can we do for you? We are praying for you. There has to be something more that we can do."

"How well do you know this town?" Cullea shifted on her chair until she faced them.

"Well enough. Why?" Taran leaned forward in turn, taking Cullea's phone. She scrolled through the photos. "Who are these? I know them from town but how did you get their photos?" She handed the phone to Payten who looked through them as well.

"We received those today. There was no letter or any explanation. It can't be the ones who are after us who sent it. It had to be someone trying to help. But with no explanation, how does that help?" Cullea was puzzled.

"We'll figure it out. The guys are meeting in the office. We'll meet here. Daci was on her way as well." Taran was on her feet and then back with a tray of food for them. "Let's eat and then pray. We'll then do what we can."

Chapter 37

Aidan was on his feet early the next morning, heading for Toryn. Toryn had not left, deep in the multiple piles of paperwork that cluttered his desk. He tapped at Toryn's door and then dropped into a chair in front of the desk.

Toryn watched him for a moment, his pen poised in the air before his hand dropped to the papers that he was working on.

"Aidan? You're troubled. What did you find out?" Toryn finally broke into Aidan's thoughts.

"I showed you the photos that Caleb and Cullea received yesterday. It was bizarre. There wasn't a letter or a note. I had a tech run them for anything hidden on them. There wasn't. There were no fingerprints on the photos and only Caleb's and Cullea's on the envelope."

"That is strange. Someone was helping us out. How does it move the case forward?" Toryn leaned forward. He had his own thoughts but he wanted to hear Aidan's thoughts first.

"It is very strange. I don't understand who but I think I have understood why. The people in the photos are involved in crime in the area, including in Oak City. I have verified that. Emma has been in touch. She's working overnight on this, she said. She has a couple of other employees working on it."

"And what did she confirm for you?" Toryn was well aware that Emma would have confirmed the identification of the people in the photos and forwarded any information on them.

"She confirmed what we were suspecting. That the head of the group is indeed looking into something that would involve audiology. He has tried in our area to some extent in the past. We just don't understand how that would work."

"I'm not sure that it would either. Cullea spoke to you about it?" Toryn thought that she would have but needed to confirm that.

"She did. That's why she was taken. She refused to help them. I fear for her. He will be coming after her. And Caleb and his team will be in the way."

"Why was Caleb targeted? Was it to do with vehicles?" Toryn watched as Aidan thought through the information.

"That could be it. How could vehicles be reprogrammed to send out messages like this?" Aidan was on his feet and back in his office. Grabbing his jacket, he headed for his car, intent on finding Caleb.

Caleb blinked through blurry eyes at Aidan. He had been asleep when Aidan pounded at his door. He stared at him before he shook his head and headed for the kitchen. He needed to make coffee and strong coffee at that to wake himself up. Aidan reached for food to make breakfast for them. This was not the first time that they had shared a meal.

"Aidan? What are you doing here this early?" Caleb set his mug back down on the table even as he shoved away his plate. He glanced at the clock. He needed to be at work in a couple of hours and those couple of hours he had planned to sleep.

"I've been working all night on those photos. I have a question for you. It relates to your work. Is there a way to do with the vehicle system what they wanted to do with hearing aids?" Aidan was trying to understand the ways of it.

Caleb shrugged. It was not something that he thought could be done but he was not an expert on that.

"I have no idea, Aidan. That's not something that I would have thought about. You would need to speak with someone who has more knowledge of that." Caleb paused for a moment before he shook his head.

"Thanks, Caleb. I'll find someone to speak with. I was just hoping that you could answer it."

Caleb walked towards the office building a few hours later, his thoughts still on what Aidan had asked. It puzzled him. He turned as he heard a voice calling his name. Paul and Thomas caught up with him.

"Caleb? You look deep in thought." Paul grinned at him.

"I am. Aidan woke me up early this morning asking me if what they wanted to do with the hearing aids could be done with vehicles." Caleb held the door open for the other two.

"That's an interesting thought." Thomas headed for his office to drop off what he had in his hands and then was back beside them. "So, we have no team in today. It's our training day. How be we spend time on

---

this instead?" He looked up to find Don watching them.

"What's up, fellows?" Don pointed to the conference room.

"Caleb is trying to figure out how they would set up vehicles to go what they want to do with hearing aids." Paul dropped his jacket on the chair that he favoured.

"Is that right? And now we need to look into that?" Don nodded. This would move along the investigation, he decided.

"We do. But first, we need to pray." Joshua's hand rested for a moment on Caleb's shoulder.

"That we will." Mark headed for his own chair, his eyes assessing his friends.

Three hours later, Caleb was on his feet and headed for the printer. He had been surprised at the information that they had found. Apparently, this was not the first time that this had been thought up.

"Caleb? What now? How do we keep you safe this time?" Don was pacing as he thought through what they could do.

"I have no idea. I don't know what to think or do anymore, Don. What do you suggest?"

"That we lock both of you away somewhere and hide the key until we find the people responsible." Mark grinned as Caleb shook his head at him. "That wouldn't work. They would just wait until you came back home."

"They would. I worry about Cullea out and about on her own during the day. It's only a matter of time until they kidnap her again. And that time would be when she would not come back to us." Caleb paced away, heading for his office, his phone out to call Cullea.

Cullea turned from the front door. Her parents were there as were Payten and Taran. She had no idea what they wanted but they all seemed to be on a mission of some kind. Cowan turned to his daughter, holding up a folder.

"Here, Cullea. This is what we've found. We need to go over it all."

Cullea shrugged. She was tired of looking at information and trying to make sense of it all. She just wanted to disappear and not appear in her life anymore.

"What do you have there, Dad?" She took the folder but didn't open it at first. She studied her father, seeing the concern that he was trying to hide. Looking in the folder, Cullea slowly leafed through the papers. She nodded. Her father had done it again. *Lord, let this be what we need to solve this. It may mean putting ourselves out there. That scares me, Lord, but I know that You are here and know the end.*

Chapter 38

A week later, Cullea turned from the bread aisle in the grocery store. She was shopping for herself and Caleb but didn't really feel in the mood. Caleb had called her earlier, simply to tell her that he loved her. He was planning on being home late that afternoon. It had become a habit for them to spend their evenings together just in talking with one another and then in Bible study and prayer.

She turned as she heard a voice beside her. She frowned, not recognizing the man who stood there for a moment.. Cullea looked around and pushed her cart away, heading for where more people were shopping.

Micah sighed. He was one of Abe's security team who had met Cullea and needed to speak with her. Caleb had told him where to find her and was heading that way as well. It just wasn't going the way that Micah had planned. Abe had sent him to speak with her. He was the only one not involved in the training that day and was free to head to Oak City.

Caleb stood beside Micah, a slightly amused look on his face. He had watched as Cullea walked away. He was glad that she had.

"Run away on you, Micah?" Caleb grinned at his friend.

"That she did. And I'm glad that she did. It shows that she is taking steps to protect herself." Micah walked towards her, Caleb at his side.

Cullea jumped as she felt arms around her and then relaxed back against Caleb. Even though they were out in public, she cherished his feelings towards her.

"Okay, sweetheart?" Caleb couldn't stop grinning as she turned around.

"I am." Her eyes moved past him to Micah. "And just who are you?"

Micah grinned in turn.

"I'm Micah. I work for Abe. I am also a friend of Caleb's. We've met before. You did right, Cullea, by moving away from me."

"I see. I'm shopping, Caleb. And just why are you here when you shouldn't be?" Cullea challenged him, seeing the slight smile still on his face.

"Abe called and asked where you were. That's how Micah found you. Don told me to come over here and protect Micah."

"Protect Micah and not protect me? I need to have a talk with him." Her phone was out as she sent off a text to Don. She stared at his response before shaking her head. Men! She would never understand them.

Caleb gathered up her bags of groceries after she had arrived home. Micah had disappeared and walked around the house, his security training kicking in. Something felt off and he was determined to find out just what it was. His phone was out as he called Aidan. Micah had found what had puzzled him. He turned and walked back to the front of the house, entering it and then walking through the house as well.

Cullea stood and watched him before she shrugged and turned to put her groceries away. Caleb stood in the hallway and watched Micah, knowing what he was doing.

"What did you find outside, Micah?" Caleb stopped him from walking past him.

"There's a problem outside of your home." Micah watched Cullea as she moved around in the kitchen. "And that's concerning."

"It is. Aidan is on his way?" Caleb had no doubt that Micah would have reached out to him.

"He is. He thought it would be about an hour or so. What can I do for you two in the meantime?"

"Tell us why you're here." Cullea had appeared beside Caleb, a frown on her face. "And I want to know what you found outside." When Micah didn't respond quickly enough, Cullea almost ran for the back door and the outside. She searched as had Micah, stopping as she saw the objects that he had found. "What are those?"

Caleb had run after her, his arms coming around her. He followed her finger as it pointed at the back of the house before he drew her away and back inside. Caleb knew what it was. Someone had piled up debris against the house. He figured that was done while Cullea had been out and that they were waiting for night to fall to set it alight.

Cullea spun to stare at the door. She was angry. She knew that she had to give God her anger but for now she felt justified in her feelings. Cullea moved away from Caleb, not seeing that his arms dropped back to his sides. He was worried about her. Micah watched the couple, not happy that Cullea had run from the house. That could have ended badly, he knew.

"Micah, I know what my team would do. What do you suggest?" Caleb's quiet voice brother through the silence in the room.

"What would I do? What would my team do? That's a good question. For starters, we would pack up and move from here. We would find a safe house to keep our protectee away from danger." Micah's eyes were on Cullea, who had turned to watch him, her arms folded across her abdomen.

"Where would that be, Micah?" Cullea questioned him.

"That I don't know. Caleb and his team know this city better than our team does. We know the safe houses around our town. Richard knows the ones around his town. If needed, we do move to other towns. That may be what is needed here. Only you and Caleb's team will need to do that." Micah watched in sympathy as her face crumpled for a moment. "God is here, Cullea. Never doubt that. He never leaves you or forsakes you. He wants only the best for you. Sometimes, He does let us go through things."

"He does. I have seen that with Paul and Payten and Thomas and Taran." Caleb wrapped an arm around her, holding her close to him. "We'll look into that. But for now, Aidan is here and needs to speak with Micah."

Aidan studied the pile of debris and then the area around it. He pulled on gloves and reached for the envelope tucked off to one side. It was what he had expected to find but prayed that he would not. It seemed as if Micah's comment about a safe house might be the answer. Only, Aidan knew that Caleb would not take that step, not if it meant letting his team down.

Caleb stood nearby, his eyes on the scene. It reminded him of something. Only he couldn't remember just what. It would come with time, he knew. He just had to let it go.

"Aidan? A letter?" Cullea walked up to Aidan, her eyes on his hands. "And of course, there would be. What did they threaten or not threaten us with this time?"

Aidan gave a quick grin. Cullea was frustrated and angry. He knew that came with what she was going through. He just prayed that they could end it and end it that night. Only, he didn't think that would happen.

"Yes, Cullea, a letter. Let's go back inside and I'll take a look at it." Aidan pointed towards the back door. "Inside and now, Cullea." His hand reached for her arm, forcing her to move at a rapid pace towards the door and then inside.

———

Chapter 39

Two days later, Caleb stared at the vehicles that had appeared suddenly and now surrounded his truck, forcing him to move in a way that he had no desire to go. He was glad that Cullea was tucked away with both sets of parents. He didn't know where she was. Richard had appeared with his team and whisked them away. Caleb was frustrated beyond what he had ever been frustrated.

Forced to a stop on road outside of Oak City, Caleb waited for something to happen. He would not make a move on his own. His hand rested on the gear shift even as his foot kept the brake pedal pushed to the floor. He was just waiting for enough of an opening and opportunity to escape. He just didn't see it happening.

The trucks surrounding him did not move. It was as if they were waiting for orders. Caleb was patient, his eyes in constant movement. The trucks began to move again, forcing Caleb's truck into movement. He was growing frustrated and desperate to get away. That wasn't seeming to happen.

Caleb slowed his truck and forced the truck behind him to slow. He spun his steering wheel and floored the accelerator, speeding away. He left a scene behind him that showed the trucks slamming to a stop and then trying to jockey around to follow him. He turned off onto a side road and then turned onto another one that would lead him back the way that he had just come. He knew the area quite well.

Pausing for a moment, Caleb turned back towards Oak City, not seeing any of the vehicles. His phone was out as he called for help. He just prayed that help would reach him in time. He really didn't know where the trucks had gotten to but he suspected that they were still in the area and on the hunt for him.

Concentrating as he was on finding the men and then avoiding them, Caleb didn't see the truck that raced towards him from behind. He saw the vehicle far too late to avoid the truck before it slammed into the driver's side back corner of his own truck. He lost control of his own truck, to his horror. He saw the ditch heading towards him before the truck rolled and rolled again, landing on the passenger's side. The truck that had rammed him paused for a moment before it sped away. Dust and debris from the ditch floated gently back to the ground. The silence that had ensued was broken again by the calls of nature as they came back.

Caleb didn't move from where he slumped forward, only held in his seat by his seatbelt. He didn't rouse at all. Blood dripped down from a slash across his forehead, landing on his arm and then the steering wheel.

Aidan was on a hunt. He had grabbed the call when it came in. Worried about his friend and the circumstances that he had found himself in, Aidan was on a search. Patrol officers were also searching for Caleb's truck. Toryn had been on his way home from a day out and picked up the call as well. He stopped at the side of a road, frowning. He knew the area and was afraid for Caleb.

Toryn drove forward slowly, watching both sides of the road. Then his brakes were slammed on. He shoved the truck into park and was out of it, running towards the side of the road. Toryn had found Caleb's truck. Bending over to stare through the shattered windshield, Toryn drew in a deep breath. His phone was out as he called it in, requesting paramedics, officer support, and a tow truck. He then carefully worked to remove the windshield. Toryn reached to check on Caleb's vitals and drew a deep breath of relief. Caleb was alive. He just didn't know how badly his friend was hurt.

Aidan pulled to a stop, staring at the truck, and was then running towards it. Toryn's hand stopped him back from it. They watched as the fire department and paramedics worked to free Caleb and then assess him. The lead paramedic walked towards the two officers, a frown on his face.

"What happened? This isn't Caleb to roll his truck. And there is damage on the back left panel." He turned to look at the truck. "It wasn't from the accident. I would suggest that he was run off the road." He walked back to Caleb, leaving the two officers to stare at one another and then at Caleb's truck.

"It has to be that, Toryn. Caleb is too careful in how he drives. Even if he has to speed for his work, he takes care." Aidan walked towards the truck, assessing what the paramedic had seen. Toryn walked beside him.

"It's true, Aidan. That didn't come from the accident. It looks as if the truck rolled a couple of times." Toryn stepped back to study the ground and then the truck.

"I would say that. We'll have the accident reconstructionist team out to have a look at it." Aidan's phone was out to request them.

"Head on in after him, Aidan. I'll stick around here for now." Toryn paused. "We'll need to bring his parents and Cullea back."

"That we do. I wouldn't want to be the one who didn't tell Cullea." Aidan's thoughts turned to the lady. "I know that they are married. I just don't know how Cullea with react with this news.."

"They are. And they both worry about each other too much. We'll get them together.." Toryn watched closely as Aidan walked away, following the stretcher that held Caleb.

Cullea stared in horror as Richard's hands on her arms held her upright. She was in shock. She had not expected Richard to approach her as he had, to tell her that Caleb had been injured in an accident. Richard knew that he had to get Cullea to Caleb and also his parents as well.

"An accident? How?" Cullea was in shock, not feeling Richard's hand turning her towards the door.

"He was run off the road, Cullea, and is in the hospital. We need to get you and his parents there. And your parents will be there as well." He tucked her into a vehicle, Naomi and Timothy beside her. Richard was behind the wheel, and a detective friend, Bill Buckley, sitting in the front passenger's seat.

Cullea was silent, her prayers on her beloved Caleb. She was so afraid that he would die before they had even had a chance to begin their lives together. Naomi's hand rested on hers, bringing comfort. At times, she could hear a whispered prayer from Timothy.

Calum and Caiti were silent as Lily, another detective friend of Richard's, drove them towards Oak City. Cowan and Casee were with Stephen and Silver in another vehicle. Richard worried about so many vehicles but he also was a realist. They didn't have any choice in this though.

Cullea was through the door into the waiting room, headed for the clerk to see if she could find Caleb. She sighed. It was not possible at that point, she was told. She would be called when she could. Cullea turned to find Caiti reaching to hug her before turning them to find seats. Neither lady saw the men milling around them, protesting them. Casee wrapped an arm around her daughter as well. None of the ladies spoke, choosing to spend their time in prayer. The two fathers walked outside with Caleb's team surrounding them. Richard's team watched from the sidelines, keeping an eye on the passerby's and the vehicular traffic.

Chapter 40

Three days later, Caleb moved cautiously through their home. He had tried to send everyone away, wanting to be on his own. He knew that Cullea was in the kitchen, working on a light meal for them. Her parents had refused to leave as had his parents. He couldn't fault them on that. Caleb knew that they didn't want to be away from him. He didn't want to be away from them.

Cullea watched him before she moved into his space, wrapping her arms around him. She had been so afraid that he would not survive. To have him walk away from the hospital with only minor injuries had been what they all felt had been God protecting them. They had talked the night before. They were married but they still felt as if they should have done it differently. They had talked briefly about what to do. Caleb didn't know that Cullea had reached out to Gideon, their pastor, that morning and asked some questions, questions that Gideon had been very glad to answer.

"You're sure, sweetheart?" Caleb was so afraid for her, having gone through what he had just gone through. She had just told him her plans.

"I am. I was so afraid that you would die. Until I saw you, that is. Your parents were really worried as well." Cullea leaned against him, afraid to let him go but afraid to have him stay.

"I know, sweetheart. I understand your fear. I have the same fear." Caleb turned her towards his office. "I have something for you." Caleb reached to slide a beautiful emerald ring on her finger. "We married so quickly, sweetheart. I just wish that it had been different. I just glad that you're mine."

"I know, Caleb. I just want what time we have together. That's all." She leaned against him, his kiss planted on her cheek.

"Okay, we'll make plans then. Now, we need to eat and then work on our mystery." Caleb turned her towards the kitchen where he could hear their parents.

"No, you need to rest."

"I can rest when we solve this and I think that we are near that." Caleb was adamant about that.

"I know, but for now, you will rest." Cullea was just as adamant.

"Okay, then. I'll rest but we will work on it tonight. We are close to finding the men and women responsible and the why's." Caleb agreed somewhat reluctantly.

Calum watched his son closely, trying to assess what he was thinking. He didn't know if it was the danger that he had just been in or something else, but Caleb had changed to some degree. He didn't know how it would end. He was afraid that he would lose his son to the men and that Cullea would die as well.

Two hours later, Caleb looked up as he heard hammering at his door. He rose to walk that way, groaning as he did so. The soft tissue injuries that he had suffered early that week were hitting him hard that night. He didn't need anyone else around. Cullea and his parents were enough. Her parents had left for the house that she had been renting and that John had been in no hurry to take back from her.

The shattering of the wooden door startled them all. Caleb turned back towards Cullea and his family, intent on moving them out of the house and hopefully to safety. He didn't make it. Caleb was tackled and taken down to the floor where he lay there with a foot on his lower back. He was able to turn his head to find Cullea. She was standing nearby, her hands covering her mouth and stifling the cry that she had been about to utter. He could see his parents, his father's arm around his mother. Caleb groaned quietly. The shock of hitting the wooden floor had jarred him. It was not what he had needed.

Hauled to his feet, Caleb reached for Cullea, drawing her to him and wrapping an arm around her to hold her tight to him. He glared at the men who had entered, realizing that they were the same men who had taken them captive all that time ago at the beginning of their adventures.

"What do you want?" Caleb went on the offensive. He had a feeling that they were waiting for someone and would not answer until that man or woman appeared. He could only pray that they survived and that his security system had picked up the breach of his door. Caleb could not be certain of that. He wasn't sure that his security system had been set. He didn't think that it had been.

Calum watched his son and then the men. His eyes narrowed. He knew the men and had known them for years. He also knew that they were involved in crime in their town. The Allans had not been very circumspect about their activities. Calum's arm tightened around his wife. He could feel the shudders of fear running through her.

Caleb's eyes raised as he heard other footsteps and sighed. *This is it, isn't it, Lord? How do we manage to get out of this situation? I don't want to lose Mom or Dad or Cullea. I just don't see how we'll survive. This is when You'll need to step in and defend us.*

"Well, Caleb. We finally see one another. You will work with me, both you and Cullea. I have plans that only you can make come true." Ivan Watson stood in front of Caleb. His rotund body showed his love of fine food and wine and liquor. He was prominent in town but was not liked at all. That had always galled him. He thought that he was so important but no one else seemed to think so.

Watson stood in front of Caleb, his beady eyes narrowed as he studied the younger man. He didn't see the fear on his face or in his bearing that he usually saw. HIs eyes turned to Cullea and saw the same attitude. Neither were afraid of him. Watson was used to that and fed off of it. He then turned to Calum and Caiti. Neither one of them showed the fear that they should have been.

Watson couldn't understand that. He thrived on the fear that he caused. Even the people that worked for him feared him. He was used to working that way.

"I don't think so, Watson. We will never work for you. And that is a fact. You won't be free much longer, I can guarantee you that." Caleb's body swayed from the blow that Watson directed at him, only Cullea's arm around him keeping him on his feet.

Caiti gave a small scream which she stifled quickly as Watson spun towards her. He studied them before he nodded. They would work for him as well. He had always been envious of Calum and the respect that he had in town. Watson craved that but never had it.

Caleb brushed at his face, the physical pain less than the pain that he was feeling in his heart. He was so afraid that Cullea and his parents would be killed. And he didn't know if he could live with that. All he could do was to petition God to defend them and send help to them. He just didn't know ion it would be in time.

Pacing back and forth in front of the two couples, Watson rubbed at his arm. An old injury from when he was a teenager was beginning to bother him more and more. He didn't realize that cancer was eating away inside him and would soon take his life. He was too concerned about being the top one in town and being respected.

Moving quietly, Aidan crept towards the shattered front door. Don had appeared just after it had been kicked in, worried about Caleb. He had reached for his phone to call it in. He now waited near his truck, the team gathering around him. Payten, Taran, and Daci were as were Cowan and Casee. All of them were worried and anxious, able to do nothing more than pray for them. And they were all confident that God would indeed honour their prayers.

The officers moved in around the house, careful in how they placed their feet so as not to make any noise and alert the men inside that they were there and would soon have them all in custody.

Aidan listened to the words that Watson was spewing. He didn't know that the officers were outside or perhaps he might have been more circumspect. Somehow, Aidan doubted that. He knew the man to be arrogant and angry. He just had no idea why.

Creeping closer to the men inside, the officers took them into custody and led them away. Aidan stood behind Watson, listening as he continued to spew words, telling the two couples exactly what they would be doing for him. He shook his head before he reached out a hand, capturing one of the man's wrists. Watson's wrists were locked into handcuffs before he even realized that he stood alone facing the couples. His anger raged at Aidan as he turned to face him, trying to tackle him and falling flat on his face as Aidan stepped to one side.

Hauled to his feet, he was shoved forward by Aidan towards the waiting officers. He was taken away, protesting the whole time, as Aidan watched.

Caleb's arms tightened around Cullea, tears on both their faces. Calum and Caiti moved in on them, wrapping them into a group hug. Aidan had to turn away, his own emotions raw. He nodded at the investigating officers and the crime scene techs as they moved in. He turned to the two couples, simply pointing to the doors.

The waiting friends and family watched as the two couples emerged from the house and then separated to give their statements. They had to wait, knowing this was a necessary step. They just didn't want to.

Cullea turned as she felt an arm around her. Their statements were finished. Caleb swept her into a tight hug, not willing to let go. He finally turned her to where her parents were waiting.

Don stopped Caleb with a hand on his shoulder. He studied the red mark on Caleb's face, knowing that he had willingly taken a blow to spare the others.

"Caleb? What happened?"

"Watson showed up, is what happened. He was determined to make all of us work for him. He was not taking no for an answer. He had these plans that he had in place that he wanted us to fulfill for him and that meant using us to do so. We'll talk later, Don. For tonight, we need to find somewhere to decompress. And we'll need to find someone for us all to speak with. It has been a huge trauma for them."

"We'll do that. For now, head off to your parents. Cullea's parents will go as well. Talk to the guys and then head off." Don walked away, his eyes on the house. He didn't know if Caleb would want to continue living there but time would tell. He would arrange for a new door to be installed that night.

Cullea turned at last from the window in her childhood bedroom. She was afraid. They had agreed to meet at her parents' home but she wasn't sure that was such a good idea. She knew that everyone was asleep or she prayed that they were. Cullea crept down the stairs and to the kitchen. She needed a cup of tea to soothe her. She just wasn't sure that it would.

Caleb watched her for a moment before he just moved in on her and cradled her to him. He could feel the tears when they started and his own tears fell. His lady had been frightened and frightened badly. That was not acceptable in his eyes.

"Okay, sweetheart?" He finally spoke.

"I think so. Is it over, Caleb?" She leaned back up to look up at him.

"It is, I think. It will take a few days for Aidan and his team to sort it all out but they will. Then, he'll meet with us just to go over the investigation with us. Couldn't sleep?" He grinned down at her.

"No, I couldn't. I was hoping that a cup of tea would help but I'm not sure that it will." She turned to make her tea and reached for the coffee pot to pour a cup of coffee for him.

"Let's sit outside for a while, sweetheart. I need to be out in the open and just feel the breeze. Sometimes, a soft breeze reminds me of the breath of God breathing on me. It brings me peace."

Cullea looked up at him as she sat, a frown on her face for a moment.

"I never thought of it like that. It's a good way to think of it." She cuddled down against him. "We need to set a date for that party, Caleb."

"We do. This Saturday?" He grinned as she stared at him, mouth open for a moment. "Not soon enough?"

"No, it's not that. I just wasn't sure if you wanted to go ahead with it or not."

Caleb kissed her, a hand on her cheek.

"I do. And I would re-marry you tonight if we could. We'll see Gideon tomorrow and see what dates he can give us."

They grew quiet, content to be with him and in the presence of their Lord. It was not long before Cullea slept, fatigue driving her to that. Caleb slept as well, not meaning to but the pain and stress took their toll on his body.

Cowan found them the next morning, surprised to find them outside. He roused them and sent them to clean up. Others would be there soon and they needed to be ready to face the day. He stood, his face turned up to the morning sky. It was going to be a bright and sunny day, one that they could thank God that they were still there to face.

———

A week later, Aidan tracked them all down at Calum and Caiti's place. They were deep in the plans for the party and simply welcomed him into the planning. He shook his head. That was not his place. His place was to let them know exactly what Watson had been up to.

Caleb turned to him at last, studying his friend before he spoke.

"Aidan? What can you tell us that can be released?"

Aidan nodded, knowing that Caleb was being cautious in his words.

"That's a good question, Caleb. All right, folks. This is what we have discovered. Watson had this idea that he could control people through the sound system in their vehicles or through hearing aids. He thought that by doing this, he could drive them into crime. We are still working through what all he wanted them to do. But we can tell you that he was deep in many crimes. Caleb? Cullea? God protected you two in a mighty way. He just wanted respect from the town and didn't have it. Jealousy drove him to do what he did. And the Allans are related to him in a distant way. He used them as well."

None of them were surprised at all. It was what they had expected. The only thing that no one could really determine is why he had been driven to live the life he did, other than sin. He wasn't saying and no one around him knew.

Three weeks later, Caleb turned in the basement of the church, searching for Cullea. She was there, beautiful in her wedding dress. He was glad that she had chosen to wear it one once to share their second ceremony with all their friends and family. She looked up and smiled at him. He grinned back before he felt a hand on his shoulder. Don stood there, watching as Daci moved towards Cullea. The two ladies had become fast friends, Payten and Taran in their group.

"Caleb? How are you?" Don waited patiently for his friend to speak.

"I'm getting there, Don. Counselling is helping. So are all of you. Richard and his team and Abe and his team are willing to talk to us at any time of the day or night. That kind of support is what gets you through."

"That it does. I'm happy that you and Cullea are married. For a while there, I didn't know if you two would survive to do that. We could all see that you were a couple from the start. God protected and defended you both. Now, I understand that we get to party a bit?" Don grinned before he moved towards the four ladies, hugging each one but holding on just a little bit longer to Cullea. She was a wonderful addition to their family, he thought, bringing just what they needed from her and her personality. His team was just opening up to let their ladies in.

Don walked away for a moment, turning to watch his team. Three of them were married now.

That was half of his team. His eyes found Joshua and Mark, standing shoulder to shoulder, laughing at the teasing that Daci was throwing at them. They squabbled at times like siblings, he thought, but they were there for one another.

His attention turned next to the two sets of parents and nodded. Both sets were taking on the men as additional family members. That was so appreciated, he thought. Aidan and Kaelen stopped beside him, one on either side, but words were not necessary between the three friends. They could to some degree understand what the others were thinking. Don knew that they were all just relieved and thankful that Caleb and his Cullea were safe and happy.

Caleb claimed Cullea from her friends and drew her away for a walk outside the church. They wandered among the tombstones, Caleb heading for where his grandparents were buried.

"My grandparents would have loved you, Cullea. You remind me of my grandmothers and in a good way. Their character was similar to yours." He stared down at her for a moment before he kissed her. "Have I told you today that I love you?"

"You have and you can continue to do that." Cullea was content. God had protected and defended them against their enemies. They still needed to face them in court but that was weeks away.

Together they walked back towards the church, hand in hand with one another. They could hear the laughter of their families and friends and smiled. Caleb reached to kiss his bride once more, her beauty warming his heart. She was exactly who he needed and she told him that he was her ideal of a knight of God.

Cullea snuggled closer to her fellow. She had dreamed of being a lady in days long ago and having a knight ride in to save her. God had known her dreams and her wants and wishes. He had provided just who she needed. Cullea's thanks rose daily to Him. He had defended both Caleb and herself in their adventure. Now, it was their turn to spread the knowledge of Him to others. Cullea had been convinced to return to her work at the hospital and she was glad to do that. Cae

They had no idea what life would bring to them. Calum and Cullea just knew that God was on their side. He had a plan for their lives already mapped out. They would follow His leading, knowing that He had already walked the path before them.

———

Thank you for choosing to read the story of Caleb and Cullea. They were really forthcoming with their story until the last few days. Then, they could not tell it fast enough. It is always a challenge to get the characters to talk. And I always ask what their story is as I start to write.

Through it all, they knew that God was their Defender. He protected them during their adventure. They learned to trust in a deeper way.

God desires that we turn to Him no matter what we are going through. He delights in our lives and in bringing to fruition our hopes and dreams. It is difficult as a human to truly understand the breadth and depth of God's love for us. He is our Defender in life. We find it difficult to understand that and to step back to allow Him to be just that.

There were once more characters who walked into the story. Abe and Emma and his team are in the *His Guardian* series. Richard and his team are in the *His Protectors*. Andrew and his Phoebe tell their tale in *The Potter's Hands*. There were others who moved through in the background. My characters just can't stay in their own stories. Blackie and his Julia's story is part of the *Mistletoe Treasures* series.

May God richly bless you as you walk the path that He has chosen for you. It is not going to be easy. There will be times that you want to turn and run and not walk forward. Don't be afraid to tell God how you

feel. He already knows but He desires that we talk with
Him and tell Him that.

    Ronna

213

www.ingramcontent.com/pod-product-compliance
Lightning Source LLC
Chambersburg PA
CBHW061300210726
48293CB00003B/1046